Ka

Imari Rogan

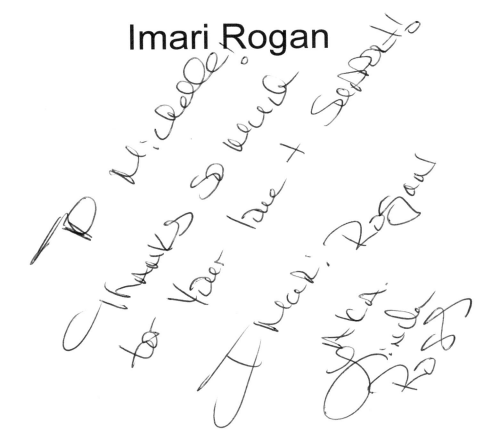

Cover Design: Bea Jackson

Published by G Publishing, LLC

ISBN: 978-0-9998578-4-7

Library of Congress Control Number: 2018960784

Printed in the United States of America

Dedication:

To my Lord and Saviour Jesus Christ! I am
nothing without you!
Thank you for the inspiration!

To my husband T,
your love, patience, and Godly wisdom is
phenomenal! Thank you from the bottom of
heart!

To my sister Garnett,
what a beautiful gem you are! Words can't
express the love I have for you! To the moon
and back!

To my nieces, Yvette, Griselda and Anika,
look at God! So grateful and blessed that you are
in my life!
I love all of you unconditionally!!

To my aunt-in-love, Mary Ann Shall,
You were loved by many and appreciated by all.
Your presence is truly missed. Rest in heaven
beautiful angel!

Acknowledgments

To my husband T, who stood behind me the entire time, listening, coaching, pushing and praying for me to do my best! So many days I was mentally and physically exhausted, but you encouraged me anyway. Thank you for believing in me and never letting me forget that all things are possible to them that believe. I love you!!

To Amber Burrell, my beautiful God daughter and treasured friend, who sacrificed her time and efforts toward this book. I can't thank you enough for your prayers, your support, your critique, and your obedience to our Heavenly Father. I pray that God's blessings over shadow you! I love you to infinity and beyond!

To Roz and Pops,
You've inspired me in ways that you can't even imagine. Thanks for loving me without walls.

To Darcel Willis, who pushed me to the limit to finish the book! Thanks so much for your support! Love you!

To Carolyn Goston, my sister from another mother. Your motivation and listening ears have been truly appreciated. Love you so much!

To Tracy Bowman, my forever friend who has always been there for me. Thank you for always believing in me and for always cheering me on! I love you very much!

To Patricia Barthwell, my editor. Thank you so much for your time and patience for this project. I know it wasn't easy by far but you did it!! Lol!

Finally to all of my readers. I truly hope that you enjoy reading this book as much as I did writing it. Thank you in advance for all of your support. I would also love to hear your feedback. Please feel free to send me an E-mail at imarirogan@yahoo.com

Enjoy!!!!

1

Kashi would never forget the first time that she saw Reuben. She was standing at the bus stop under the shelter, when Reuben entered and stood on the opposite side. It had been a long day of classes at the local university, where she was completing her second month of classes, as a Junior. He was one of the best looking guys she had ever laid her eyes on. As soon as she noticed him, she felt instant attraction. She was drawn to him. She was intoxicated. Hundreds of red flags began to pop up in her mind. She didn't even know him. Actually, she knew absolutely nothing about him and yet she felt instantly connected to him. From a realistic standpoint, this man was off limits. He was way off limits because of tradition and ethnicity. Why did he have to be African American, when she was Indian?

"Oh well," she thought, as she told herself to calm down and stop overreacting. There was no point in looking at him any further, but as she stood there cradling her backpack on one shoulder and her shoulder bag on the other, she was totally unaware she was staring at him. Kashi was mesmerized. She noticed his beautiful, brown, almost flawless complexion, his full black eyebrows and somewhat slender nose. But those lips! They were full, luscious and sexy looking lips that seemed to be begging to be kissed! Oh my gosh she thought!! What's wrong with me?! I've never had thoughts like this! And yet she couldn't stop herself. Then she noticed his height. He must have been at least 6'2 and his muscles seemed to bulge through the jacket he was wearing. She assumed that he worked out at the gym every single day.

As Reuben stood in the corner of the shelter, he was engrossed in whatever he was reading. It looked like a college textbook, so Kashi assumed he was a student on campus, just as she was. Maybe he sensed her staring at him, because he suddenly closed the book, tucked it away in his backpack and looked in her direction. He smiled slightly at her. Embarrassed, she quickly looked away and pretended to be engrossed with the scenery around her. She forced herself to think about how quickly the weather had changed. Summer had come and gone all too quickly and fall was approaching. The trees had already turned from green to brown, scattering golden, rust colored leaves on the ground below. Kashi could only imagine what another winter would bring. Winters in Nebraska were known to be very harsh and she wasn't looking forward to it. He moved from his corner of the shelter closer to where she was standing. Now she could smell him. Dear God! He smelled so good!! Still pretending to stare at the scenery and the traffic whizzing by, she heard him say

Imari Rogan

hello. Shaking like a leaf inside, she tilted her head slightly in his direction. "Hello," she replied. It was almost a whisper but his voice was deep and sexy. Now it was his turn to stare at her. She shyly looked at him and he seemed to be enjoying the moment. He smiled warmly at her and introduced himself.

"I'm Reuben and whom might you be?" Is this really happening? she asked herself. Did he really just walk over here and introduce himself to me? "I'm Kashi." "Kashi," as he paused for a moment "That's such a beautiful name. A beautiful name for a beautiful woman." He stared directly into her eyes. Feeling her face flush, she quickly turned away "Thank-you," she said softly. She was so embarrassed. She wasn't used to the opposite sex being so straightforward with her. Up until college, she had basically lived in her own little private world. One that was almost non existent except for family and close friends. "I assume you attend the university?" he asked. "Yes," she responded. "What are you studying?" "Pre Med and you?" "Law," he answered. She was impressed. She didn't know why but she was really impressed. Maybe she didn't think that black people were interested in things like that. She knew that her thinking was totally biased, hypocritical and somewhat stereotyped and she chided herself for it. They made small talk about their classes and she shared with him how she wanted to be a doctor. She also mentioned that both of her parents were obstetric gynecologists. He neither seemed surprised nor taken aback by the information given but seemed to take it for granted. Perhaps another stereotype. They both agreed that they were on the road to success. He shared with her that his father was a lawyer, who owned his own law firm. He also said that he hoped to work for his father's firm sometime after graduation, which would be in the next year or so. As Kashi listened to him talking, she began to realize that in the short amount of time they were speaking, she was really enjoying the conversation and his company. It had taken her mind off of her current situation. A situation that she had been forced into. A hopeless and depressing situation that almost brought tears to her eyes.

****

Studying to be a doctor had not been an easy task for Kashi thus far. The decision to be a doctor had not been her first choice but she chose that, just to please her family. Everything that she did and every decision she made was based around her family and their wishes and beliefs. Her personal needs and preferences had been pushed aside because of them. Her life had already been mapped out. Every single detail of it, including whom she would marry. That was because Kashi's parents followed the tradition of arranged marriages and Logan Roy had been their first and only choice. It had long been decided, prior to her birth that she would be given in marriage to him. It was tradition, and while most American Indian families no longer held fast to this rule, Kashi's parents seemed to be the last of the traditionalists. The Logan and Pattel families were best friends and had met as neighbors while living in India. Logan was the first born to the Roy Family, followed by two more children, including a boy and a girl.

The Pattel family was still anxiously trying to conceive and had almost given up hope, when it was discovered that they were expecting. They crossed their fingers and hoped for a girl and when Logan turned 10, Kashi was born. Both families were thankfully overjoyed and the decision for the children to be married was finalized.

When the Roy family moved to America to pursue better careers, the Pattel family followed. Both parents from each perspective family, opened up their own private medical practice and America truly became the land of opportunity for everyone involved. Once in America, the Pattel Family welcomed two more children. Kashi became a big sister to a set of twins, a boy and a girl, which totally took the Pattel family by surprise. Kashi was 11 when the twins were born and the adjustment was more than awkward for her and embarrassing for her parents, who were approaching 50. Nonetheless, as Kashi and Logan grew up together, one thing was crystal clear. She DID NOT like Logan! Matter of fact, she loathed him! He was 10 years her senior, she didn't like his personality, she wasn't crazy about his looks and she just didn't LIKE HIM! He wasn't ugly by a long shot. He was fairly nice looking but he just wasn't her type. She wasn't sure what her type was but Logan definitely wasn't it, even though he was a successful doctor, who specialized in the field of Gastroenterology and was well established, with his own private practice at 30. What each family had not perceived however, was the fact that Kashi hated Logan.

Logan, on the other hand, was crazy about Kashi. He loved everything about her. The two had started dating when Kashi had turned 18 and now two years later, the wedding was set for next June, just after Kashi 's 21st birthday. She had argued with her parents countless times telling them how unhappy she was with their choice but she had always been met with strong opposition. His side of the family wouldn't listen to her either. Neither family could understand Kashi's sadness and resentment. They thought that it was blessing to be able to marry someone of Logan's demeanor and social status. They even

Imari Rogan

expressed how there were hundreds of young Indian women, who would jump at the chance to marry someone like Logan. Kashi felt like telling both families that all these other women could have him but instead decided to keep quiet.

It was a no win situation. If she chose to go against their wishes, she may risk losing a relationship with both sides. She knew her parents would disown her, so she decided to go through with the marriage plans and just be miserable for the rest of her life. She couldn't even picture growing to love Logan. If she didn't even remotely love him by now, she knew that she never would.

And now as the conversation between her and Reuben continued, she allowed herself to relax. It was refreshing to engage in a conversation with another man other than Logan. It was strange how relaxed she felt. All too soon the bus pulled up and they both got on together and paid their fare. She took a seat closest to the window and he sat down next to her. "How far are you going?" he asked. "About 15 miles south of here. I live in the Shadows Subdivision with my parents." "Oh yeah, I know the area, my parents almost bought a condo in that sub too but decided they wanted something a little bigger, so we moved to the Woodbridge Estates. Kashi raised her eyebrows slightly. The Woodbridge Estates contained million dollar homes and housed some of the wealthiest residents in the state. Many times, Kashi had dreamed what it would be like to live in one of those homes. He chuckled a little at the expression on her face. "It's not that big of a deal." A few moments passed before they spoke again. She could feel his body heat merging with hers, as they sat next to each other. Their shoulders and legs touched. She wanted to bury her head in his chest. "Kashi, may I ask you a personal question?" She snapped out of her day dream. "Sure" she said. "I love that fragrance you're wearing, what's the name of it?" Kashi thought for a moment. She normally didn't wear perfume only scented lotion. Finally she thought of it. "It's called pineapple passion, it's body lotion." She watched the corners of his mouth turn up into a sexy smile. "It smells incredible," he said. She dropped her head and nervously looked at her hands. Her heart was skipping beats. There were butterflies in her stomach and she felt the heat rise to her face.

All of a sudden, he reached over her head to ring the bell to get off the bus. She was mortified. Why did this encounter have to end so soon? "Well," he sighed, "the next stop is mine. It was very nice to meet you Kashi, I hope to see you again on campus real soon," as he smiled "Me too." she whispered. And with that, he arose from his seat and walked to the front. When the bus came to a stop, he quickly looked back over his shoulder at her and flashed her a big smile and with that he was gone.

Kashi watched him walk away as the bus pulled off and followed him with her eyes until he was out of sight. She was kind of disappointed that they had not exchanged any contact information. Would she ever see him again? The university campus was huge. What were the chances of running into him? He had told her earlier that the only reason that he was taking the bus was because his vehicle was in the shop. Maybe she should have asked for his phone number. What was she thinking? He probably wasn't even interested in her and that made her sad. But wasn't it his responsibility to pursue her? Yes, it should be and not the other way around. So much for wishful hopeful thinking. She tried to forget about Reuben the rest of the way home but it was difficult. The only thing that snapped her back to reality was when the bus reached her destination. She dragged herself off and walked the half mile to her subdivision. Before long, she felt the familiar headache coming on. Tonight was Friday night and she had a date with Logan. The customary Friday night date that would loom before her until the day she married. After that, it would not only be Friday night but EVERY night! Kashi wanted to die!

2

Reuben could hear the shouting, as he made his way up the drive way, that led to the back of the house. He inhaled deeply as he entered through the garage door and stepped into the massive kitchen. He was tired and wasn't in the mood to break up a fight between his parents. It seemed as though that lately, all his parents did was fight. He saw his mother standing at the kitchen sink, with her back to his father, who couldn't see the tears streaming down her face. His father continued the shouting even though Reuben was standing a few mere feet away from them. His father glanced in his direction and ignored his presence "I don't have to explain anything to you Catherine! I told you already that I've been faithful to this marriage and that's all you need to you know!" "I don't believe you," his mother cried, as she turned around to face her husband, who was now standing a few inches from her face. "You are a lying cheat. How else do you explain coming home all hours of the night and sometimes not at all?!"

Reuben could see the anguish and anger in his mother's face, as she stood defiantly waiting for an answer. Reuben saw what was about to happen but was too late to do anything about it. In one second flat, his father's face contorted into a monster like grimace and he slapped Reuben's

Imari Rogan

mother across the face. The slap was so hard that it sent his mother reeling to the floor. She was clutching the side of her face and crying uncontrollably, while trying to regain her composure. She looked helplessly in Reuben's direction. He took a step towards his father and snatched him by his collar. "Why did you do that dad? he screamed. "Let go of me, you have nothing to do with this!" "I have everything to do with this, that's my mother and I'm tired of you abusing her!" His father reached up and grabbed Reuben's hands from around his shirt collar. When he was free, he stepped back a bit and punched Reuben in his face. Reuben lost his balance and stumbled to the floor. "Stay out of it!" his father hissed. Reuben felt the hot liquid pouring out of his nose and realized he was now bleeding. He wiped the blood with the back of his hand. The pain was almost unbearable. He hoped that it wasn't broken. "Leave him alone!" his mother screamed, as she lay in a heap on the floor. His father looked at the both of them in disgust before storming out of the kitchen.

They both heard the Range Rover start up and screech out of the driveway. He could be heard speeding out of the sub-division. His mother had no actual proof that her husband was cheating, but Reuben had proof and didn't think he would ever have the heart to tell her. He eased himself towards his mother on the floor and took her into his arms. She cried softly. He rocked her back and forth in his arms and they cried together. He loved his mother with all of his heart and the hatred for his father was beginning to build, from all the pain and hurt he had caused his mom.

****

Reuben thought back to the fateful evening when he had discovered his dad's infidelity. It had been about three years ago, when Reuben had taken a summer job at his father's law firm working in the mailroom. Mere weeks prior to that evening, a young woman named Tina, had walked into the law firm looking for a job. She was 30 years old and desperate for work. She had the experience but her demeanor and dress were very questionable. She had strutted into the office for an interview, wearing a super tight mini skirt, an extra small blouse, super high heels and overdone makeup. Reuben remembered seeing her waiting to be interviewed, as he deposited the mail at the receptionist desk . He felt an instant dislike for Tina and was positive that his father would never hire anyone so tacky. But to everyone's surprise, his dad had whisked her into the conference room for the interview and was smiling ear to ear. That's when Reuben knew different. His father hired her on the spot, sending the entire office into a tailspin of disbelief and shock. But his father quickly shut everyone down from the idle talk and gossip floating around about his new secretary.

Tina sashayed around the office getting coffee and doughnuts for the clients, as if she owned the place and her attire had only gotten worse. After numerous complaints from both staff and clients, his father finally addressed Tina about the firm's dress code. She had no choice but to comply and started dressing in a professional matter, but little else changed. She was a slut and Reuben knew that she had it in for his dad.

Reuben tried speaking to his father about Tina and her obvious intentions. But his father only yelled at him and warned him not to check him about anything. His father confirmed that he was and always would be faithful to his mother and then he pushed Reuben out of his office and slammed the door.

It was only two weeks later, after that incident, that Reuben had finished his shift but had to return to the office. After reaching the parking lot, he realized he had left his car keys behind. Reuben let himself into the office and wasn't really paying any attention to the noises coming from the conference room. He grabbed his keys from the mail room desk and headed towards the front door. He heard the noises again and abruptly stopped to listen. It sounded like moaning. He stood like a statue and listened more intently. He noticed that the door to the conference room was slightly ajar, so as quietly and slowly as he could, he made his way to the room and peered inside. His worst fears were confirmed. Tina was lying on the side of the conference table, with her skirt hiked up above her waist and his father was penetrating her like the world was going to end. They looked like two wild animals in the heat of passion. Reuben was disgusted with the image starting to burn through his mind, as he watched them. Neither one noticed him, as he stood in the crack of the opened door. Reuben was livid! He slammed the door on purpose to let them know that they had been discovered. He ran out of the office and got into his car. He was shaking with rage. He took his fist and banged it so hard on the steering wheel that he thought it was broken.

Reuben sat in his car and took deep breaths to calm himself down. He looked up at the conference room window, which faced the parking lot where he was sitting. His father was standing in the window staring back at him looking disheveled and bewildered. Their eyes locked for a brief moment then Reuben started the Range Rover and burned rubber leaving the parking lot. He vowed never to tell his mother the information he had learned that night. He now had proof that his dad was cheating and with who.

Imari Rogan

This now gave him an edge over his father, who also knew he had been caught. And of all people to catch him in this act of infidelity, it was his son. As Reuben continued to cradle his crying mother, he vowed in his heart that if God ever blessed him with a wife, he would always be faithful to her.

3

Doctors Anna & Pasok Pattel were prominent doctors in the suburban city of Grand Island. They were happily married with seemingly no major marital problems to speak of. They were super excited about the upcoming wedding in the next few months. They hadn't planned on withholding any expenses concerning their daughter's wedding. Nothing was too good for their firstborn daughter. Jessica and Jason, the twins would be next to marry in about 10 years or so. At least that was the plan. They would allow Jason to pick a bride of his own choosing but Jessica would follow the family tradition of arranged marriage. They had yet to find a suitable husband for Jessica but they were looking among close friends and co-workers.

It was clear that the Pattel family would not have anymore children and Jessica and Jason had proven to be more than a blessing. The twins were wild about their older sister but with an 11-year age gap, it made it difficult for Kashi to relate to them, as she wished but she tried her best. She played hide and go seek with them, played video games and even read them bedtime stories. And yes, they occasionally fought but she loved them with all of her heart and their bond was inseparable. The weekends were family time. The only time that the five of them could come together as family, without any outside interruptions and spend quality time. As a rule, Kashi's parents had agreed that only one weekend per month would be utilized for on call patient emergencies. Family was first. Luckily for Kashi tonight was the beginning of a family weekend together that she was glad of because she wanted to discuss Logan with her parents again. She appreciated their efforts but she just wasn't happy. She decided for the final time that after tonight's date with Logan she would bring the issue up again on Saturday morning. She pretty much knew how the conversation would end, as it had so many times before, but she knew that she had to keep trying. Maybe one day they would listen.

On Friday evening, her date with Logan dragged by. He arrived at her door at 7 p.m., ready for dinner and a movie. He drove her to an exclusive middle eastern restaurant located downtown in the heart of the city, that was reservation only. Logan looked decent in a pair of faded jeans and a football jersey and Kashi was beautiful regardless of what she chose to wear. But since she could have cared less about the date, she purposely threw on an old faded sweater and a pair of jeans that were torn and ragged at the knees. She hoped that it would deter Logan's attention away from her. Sadly, it didn't work. Logan gasped at her beauty tonight as he always had. It was pointless to try to look tacky. Somehow, she still managed to look like a runway model. Kashi was simply beautiful. With her light brown complexion and long silky black hair that flowed beneath her shoulders, others always wondered what her nationality was. Was she Hispanic, Arabic or Filipino? It was usually her deep set eyes and chiseled nose that revealed her race to others. With a curvaceous figure and small body frame, she was able to effortlessly slip into any size 10 outfit of her choosing. While Kashi only thought of herself as ordinary, family and friends begged to differ, especially Logan. To Logan, she was EXTRAORDINARY, a true vision of loveliness.

As the waitress led them to their table, she noticed a couple of young Indian women staring at Logan, from where they were seated. She glared at them but secretly she could have cared less but the looks were disrespectful, since she was his date. They were welcome to him as far as she was concerned but it didn't matter because Logan wasn't paying any attention to them anyway. He only had eyes for Kashi. "Kashi, what's wrong? You're so distant tonight." he stated, once they were seated. I'm distant every night she thought to herself. "Nothing's wrong Logan, I've had a long day at school and I'm ready to eat and go home." "Go home after dinner?" he asked. He seemed shocked. "What about the movies and the after hours club?" Did he just hear what I told him about being tired? she thought. "No, Logan, not tonight, like I said, I'm tired," she said, matter of factly.

Kashi pretended to be engrossed with the menu, while her mind drifted back to the earlier events of the day. She thought about Reuben, the handsome young man she had met at the bus stop. A faint smile moved across her lips. Logan noticed her smile. "That's my girl, perk up a little bit" His voice snatched her back to the present and her smile instantly faded. Her eyes narrowed into slits as she glared at him. Was he dumb enough to think that she was smiling about him? "What's wrong? he asked. "I already told you," she said, just short of calling him stupid. "I'm tired!' Trying to bring some light into an already dark conversation, Logan mentioned their upcoming wedding. What an absolute horrid thing to do! His words were no sooner out of his mouth, when he realized the mistake he had made. Kashi rolled her eyes up towards the ceiling and looked in the opposite direction. How she hated this night! That's when she noticed the same two young women staring in their direction again.

"I'm ready to leave," she stated, turning her attention back to Logan. "But we haven't even had dinner yet." Logan was exasperated. "Kashi, please tell me what's wrong with you. I know that we both feel a little different about each other but I think that you can grow to love me if you would just give me a chance" He was desperate. She considered what he said for a brief moment but only for a brief moment before finally answering him with even more venom in her voice. "Logan please understand this." She spoke slowly and methodically. "I think you're a very nice young man, who has a very successful career and an even brighter future ahead of you but I don't want to be a part of it."

She was sorry as soon as she had said it. He looked really crushed. She could see the tears began to well up in his eyes.

"Logan I'm"......The waitress returned to their table with their meals and placed them on the table. "May I have the check please?" he asked. His voice was trembling. "Yes Dr. Roy but is everything okay?" The waitress glanced quickly at Kashi with an accusing judgmental look before turning her attention again to Logan. "Yes ma'am" he answered "but I have somehow lost my appetite, so could you please pack our dinners to go?" "Yes sir." The waitress looked at Kashi once more with a look of disdain before walking away. Was it that obvious to everyone around her how much she despised him? Kashi glared at the backside of the waitress, as she walked away and resisted the urge to go after her and slap her. Kashi had always been straight forward in everything that she had said and done and it was one of the qualities that Logan admired about her but it wasn't very admirable tonight. Now it was him that just wanted the evening to end. He tried to convince himself that she was just tired and needed some rest. He was sure that as time went on, she would love him the way that he loved her. He dabbed at his eyes quickly with the dinner napkin and choked back more tears. The waitress returned to their table with carry out boxes and the check. This time she didn't even look in Kashi's direction "Thank-you Dr. Roy and enjoy the rest of your evening." "WE WILL," Kashi blurted out, before Logan could answer. The waitress flipped her hair and walked away in a huff. "What's her problem?" she asked to no one in particular. "You are being rude Kashi and that's what the problem is." "Whatever," she replied. Her remorse for her earlier comment had faded away.

They walked out of the restaurant in silence and the ride home was a long slow one that felt like a library moment. She tried not to think about how bad she had hurt Logan's feelings, so instead she let her mind drift back to Reuben. He was so handsome and soft spoken. She thought about what life would be like with him. She allowed herself to imagine being on a date with him instead of Logan and how different the night could be. She imagined how she was talking and laughing and having the time of her life. She imagined their first kiss. She leaned back into bucket seats and closed her eyes. How she wished that she was with him tonight.

"Good Night Kashi" She opened her eyes and realized that she had arrived home. She glanced over at Logan and somehow managed to say goodnight. Before Logan could get out of the car and walk her to the house, she hurriedly got out and ran to the front door. She quickly let herself in without looking back. She needed to talk with her parents and she needed to talk right now!

Her mother and father were sitting in the living room watching a movie with the twins, when she came barging in. "Hey honey how was your date with Logan?" her mom asked. Kashi grabbed the tv remote off of the coffee table and flicked the television off. "Hey! Why did you do that?" screamed Jessica. Poor little Jason looked at her in bewilderment as if he knew what was coming.

"I'm sorry but twins could you please leave the room, while I speak to mom and dad alone!" The stern look on her face told them that she meant business. They both looked at their parents to protest but quietly left the room. "Kashi what is this all about?" demanded her father. "You storm in here after your date with Logan ranting and raving like a madwoman, ready to bite off both our heads." "Dad I think you already know what this is about I don't want to marry Logan!" Her father let out a long sigh and dropped his head. Her mom looked exasperated. "Honey we have been through this many many times before and it's already set. According to our traditional custom, you have to marry Logan," her mom said desperately. "Mom the only reason that I have to marry Logan would be out of respect to the both of you. There really is no law if I don't. I would only be breaking a stupid tradition".

With that, her father angrily arose from his seat on the couch and stood face to face with Kashi. He was very angry. "A stupid tradition that considers what is best for your well being!" He paused for a moment before continuing. "Before your mother and I left Pakistan some 20 years ago, we had already made that fateful decision that you hate so much. I don't need to reiterate anything to you! We know the history of the Roy family and they know ours. We know everything about each other! Our background, our history, everything! Logan is a fine young man, who is well able and willing to take good care of you and he will be an excellent provider for you. As soon as you're married you can have the home of your dreams just waiting for you. I do not understand what the problem is!! She took a deep breath and slowly enunciated every syllable before speaking. "I do not LOVE HIM!!!

Her father returned to his seat and turned the television back on, which indicated that the conversation was over. She pleadingly looked in her mother's direction but she refused to make eye contact. She just sat there staring at the floor. Okay, she thought, if they want to play hardball than all of us will play hardball. It was all about respect. She didn't want to lose the respect of her parents and disgrace them by going against tradition BUT she had a plan. One thing about Kashi Pattel that everyone knew and that was the fact that she wasn't fake. She wasn't going to pretend to be in love or even try to fall in love with someone that she despised. If everything went according to her plan, everyone would be miserable by the time that the wedding arrived. Hopefully by that time, both families would be ready to call it off. She felt the fight of opposition coming on. It was time to rumble!

Imari Rogan

4

Logan could barely focus on what he was doing. He was in the middle of an endoscopic procedure with a 70 year old patient, who complained of recurrent abdominal pain. The procedure allowed for a tube like scope to be inserted down the patient's throat. This would enable Logan to see into the stomach cavity with a light and a camera like tool to detect abnormalities. He tried to concentrate on the task at hand but the date with Kashi on Friday night had left him more than a little upset. He was uneasy the entire weekend. He forced himself to pay attention to what he was doing. He finally finished the procedure and gave the diagnostic code to his colleague. He excused himself from the room, went into his office and closed the door. He removed his gloves and washed his hands in the bathroom sink. He stepped out and slumped down into the high back chair at his desk and put his head in his hands.

He wearily looked up at the photo that was perched in the corner of his desk. It was a photo that both he and Kashi had taken for their engagement. Logan was posed standing behind Kashi with his arms around her waist. They were both smiling. He carefully studied the photo and looked into the pair of eyes that stared back at him. He wondered how she had actually felt that night. He assumed at the time that the feeling of happiness had been mutual between them. Kashi hadn't let on prior to that night that anything was wrong. But that was BEFORE that fateful night that the "incident" had occurred between them.

God, she was so beautiful he thought to himself as he studied the photo. What was he doing wrong in their relationship? Was he too blunt? Too forceful? Too pushy, what was it? They were set to be married in a few months and from the time they had spent dating, two years to be exact, they should have at least made more progress than this, from an emotional standpoint. Kashi for the most part had always been kind of cold and distant but Logan hadn't really paid it any attention until recently. In the beginning of their relationship, she was somewhat timid and shy but always polite. He was proud to know that one day she would be his wife. When they dated, he always purposely took her to public settings and events so that he could show her off as his. He wanted the world to know that Kashi Pattel belonged to him and that she was his heart. He took her to baseball games, basketball games, upscale restaurants, the movies, the theater, concerts with front row tickets, Indian dance clubs and everywhere that he could think of. He even took her on shopping excursions and purchased designer handbags and clothing for her. He showed her nothing but the utmost

Imari Rogan

respect and adorning love, so why couldn't she just love him in return?

Tears pooled in the corner of his eyes, as he thought about the prospect of losing her. It was obvious that she had been pulling farther and farther away from him, especially as of late. Before they had started dating, the only contact that they had with each other had been at family gatherings. He could remember making eye contact with her and trying to make conversation but she had always avoided him and pretended to be occupied with her friends. He figured that maybe it was because of the age gap and that once they started dating everything would change. She just needed to get to know him. On their first date, Logan showed up at her front door with a dozen roses and front row tickets to a concert for her favorite rock group. He wanted to make sure that he made a good first impression and he had. She had screamed with delight when she found out where they were going and they had a great time at the concert. Afterwards, he had even taken her out to dinner. By the time they reached the restaurant, Kashi could barely talk. Her voice was raspy from all the screaming at the concert. Nonetheless, they laughed and talked and from that moment on, they dated almost every Friday night. He loved being with her but the more they dated, the more distant she had become .

Now two years later, Kashi was miserable and she was starting to make him feel miserable. She barely spoke two words to him on their dates. She would stare into space and daydream while he was talking to her. She never really paid much attention to what he was saying and each time that he would ask her what was wrong, she would just shrug her shoulders and ask to go home. But he knew exactly what the problem was. He knew in his heart that they should have waited. Maybe if they had waited until marriage, she may not have lost the little bit of respect that she had for him. But what difference would it have made anyway if they were still going to be married? Feeling frustrated, his mind drifted back to the forbidden beautiful night. The night of the "incident".

****

It had been beautiful for him but horrible for her. It had only happened once and at this point in the relationship, he hoped and prayed that it would happen again. But deep within his heart, he was starting to give up hope. It was around six months ago when things in their relationship had gone from bad to worse. Logan decided that maybe they needed to take their relationship to the next level in order to salvage it. He thought that maybe sex would make things better but that turned out to be a drastic mistake.

Imari Rogan

He thought about the night when everything went haywire.

They had just come from the movies one Friday evening and the night was still young. He wasn't in the mood to end the date early. Not this time. "Where would you like to go now?" he had asked Kashi. "I don't really know. I'm not hungry, so maybe we should just call it a night." Without even so much as another word, they got into the car and Logan pulled out onto the freeway. He began driving in the opposite direction of home. They drove about 40 miles outside of the city limits and Kashi never asked him where they were going. He turned off of the highway and pulled into the parking lot of a beautiful excluded motel. He glanced sideways at her when he parked the car and noticed that she looked nervous. "Why are we here?" she asked. "Let me make love to you Kashi. I'm sorry for bringing you here without your permission, so we can turn around and head back home if you'd like". "No, it's okay. We're here now," she said softly. So before she could change her mind, Logan sprinted out of the car and ran into the motel lobby to check them in. He emerged five minutes later, with a set of keys dangling in his hand. He was silent as he started up the engine and drove around to their room, on the side of the building. Logan opened the door for her and led Kashi in.

The room was breathtaking. It had a huge living room with an already lit fireplace, a kitchen and an upstairs loft where the bedroom was. Logan took a deep breath as he glanced around the spacious room. He felt like a kid in a candy store. Kashi sat on the couch in the living room looking nervous. He noticed that she was trembling. "Kashi, is this your first time?" She was insulted with his question. He regretted asking it as soon as it was out of his mouth. What did he think? She was a nice girl, who was only 19 and had lived a sheltered life. How could he be so stupid to ask her something like that?' "Yes," she answered, looking offended. "I apologize for asking you that. Please forgive me." He watched her face soften. Now it was her turn to ask a question. "How did you find this place, have you been here before?" "No, but I saw it off of the highway once, on my way out of town with my parents a few years ago. I kept it in my memory bank just for us." "I see." After an awkward and lengthy silence, he reached for her hand and led her upstairs to the bedroom. Without any spoken words, they quietly undressed, climbed into the bed and slid under the covers.

He began to kiss her passionately but she stopped him in the middle. "I'm a virgin" she reminded him. "Me too," he whispered. Kashi looked absolutely shocked. "I've been saving myself for you and this moment" he replied. Now

Imari Rogan

he was even more nervous. Please don't mess this up he warned himself. This is your last chance at redemption regarding this relationship. You have to make her love you. Make it good. With neither one of them having any real experience, Logan felt like a real idiot. A 29 year old virgin. He almost laughed at himself but forced a serious look instead. This was a pivotal moment.

He kissed her for a long time and moved to her breasts. He took each nipple, one at a time into his mouth and sucked them gently. He heard her silent moans and felt his manhood stiffen. What was he supposed to do next? He was so ready for her. He glanced at her face. Her eyes were closed and she seemed to be enjoying the moment. He reached over to grab a condom from the nightstand table where he placed one earlier. He ripped the paper off with his teeth and awkwardly placed it on. At first it was backwards and than he had to start all over again. Thank God that Kashi didn't seem to notice his mistake. He was already a basket case. He mounted himself on top of her and penetrated her. She screamed in pain. He was startled and pulled out abruptly. "What's wrong? "You hurt me! " she angrily yelled "I'm sorry," he said "I told you I was a virgin. Why weren't you more careful?"

She was practically screaming at him. She looked so angry and upset and pushed him off of her. He felt so stupid and embarrassed. This was not going well at all. "I'm so sorry Kashi. Can we try again?" She angrily leaned back into the pillows and let out a long sigh. She reluctantly opened her legs, clearly unsure of what would happen next. He slowly eased himself back inside of her and began to move back and forth. At first it was slow and rhythmic but the feeling was getting intense.

He loved her so much and the feeling of having sex with her for the first time only intensified the moment. He felt his body doing things that he had never done before and making sounds that he had never made before. Yes, Logan was losing control. He felt himself moving harder and harder and faster and faster and he forgot all about his beloved Kashi.

His feelings went into selfish mode. He wanted to help himself but couldn't. He knew that he was about to reach his peak. He knew the familiar feeling from the times that he had spent alone, fantasizing about Kashi. She felt so warm and so moist. He felt the enormous pressure of his orgasm building like a faucet and he had to let it go. He slammed into her one final time and was lost in one big explosion that felt like the world had crashed. He faintly heard Kashi screaming and assumed that it had been just as good for her. He was sweating profusely as he collapsed on top of her and panted heavily. He finally rolled off of her after a minute or two and looked over at her.

Wow, that was so wonderful he thought to himself. Her arms were folded across her chest and she was staring at the ceiling. She was angry. "Kashi was everything okay?" She didn't answer him. She wrapped herself in the bed sheet and went into the bathroom and slammed the door. Logan heard the shower running but he was too exhausted to run after her and he drifted off to sleep. When she came out of the bathroom, he was still lying in the same position. When he finally awoke, Kashi was gone.

Logan jumped out of the bed in a panic and looked over the railing into the living room. He saw Kashi was fully dressed and sitting on the couch, obviously ready to leave. He took a quick shower, dressed and met her downstairs. She didn't even so much as look at him. He wondered what she was thinking. He loved her now more than ever but something had gone horribly wrong tonight. They should have waited. But how would any other night have been different from tonight?

Not a word was spoken on the ride back home. He knew that he had somehow blown it. He kicked himself again and again for being so selfish tonight. What a dumb fool he was. When they arrived at her place, he walked her to the door. She didn't say goodbye. She opened the door, went inside and closed the door in his face. During the next few dates it was business as usual. Each of them had never discussed the "incident" again.

****

Logan arose from his desk and went to stare out of the office window. The ringing phone disrupted his thoughts. "Hello, Dr. Roy speaking" "Yes Doctor Roy," replied his receptionist, "I have a Kashi Pattel on line 1." "Yes put her through" he said excitedly. His heart skipped a beat and he could not believe that she was calling him at work. She rarely if ever did that. "Yes Kashi, how may I help you?" "We have to talk." She simply said "Yes of course when?' "Can you pick me up from class this afternoon? He looked at his watch. It was 2:30 "Sure what time?" "About 4:00? "Okay that's fine, my last patient is at 3:00. I should be there no later than 4:15" "Okay I'll be waiting for you outside of building A" "Okay, I'll see you then" He hung up with a smile on his face. Wow! She wanted to talk. He hoped that it would be good news, since he needed it now more than ever.

Imari Rogan

5

Kashi's mind was made up. She was going to tell Logan that she wanted to break up with him. She just couldn't tolerate him any longer. She looked at her watch. 3:30. She had just finished her last class and decided she needed a good half an hour before facing him, so that she could gather her thoughts. She left the building feeling tense and stressed out. She dreaded how she would tell Logan that their relationship was over.

She sat down on a nearby bench, just outside of the campus building, so that Logan would be able to see her from the street when he arrived. She placed her duffle bag on the ground beside her and took a deep breath. The fall temperature was starting to drop and she shivered a bit while zipping up her jacket. Inwardly, she shivered too. The last thing that she wanted to do was break Logan's heart. He really was a decent guy who adored her but she was unable to return his feelings and it wasn't fair to Logan to keep leading him on. She knew that the breakup was inevitable and had to be done. It wasn't going to be easy.

She regretted the fact that she had made love to him. It had only complicated an already bad situation but somehow at the time she thought that it would make things better. Besides, she had been a little bit curious about what having sex would really be like. Most of her friends had lost their virginity during their teens, with their prospective husbands to be, and were set up to be married as well. Her friends were happy too, so why wasn't she? Why couldn't she just love Logan? The night that they made love, she figured that she had nothing to lose except her virginity. Why not? she had asked herself. He was going to be her husband anyway and maybe she would actually enjoy sex with him. She had been curious to find out. After that horrible night had ended, her mind had changed drastically. There was no way that she was going to marry someone, who had totally disgusted her both in and out of the bedroom.

Logan's kisses had disgusted her. They were wet and sloppy and his hands had felt clammy and cold against her skin and while she was no expert at sex, she was more than sure that he had climaxed way too quickly. After the deed had ended, she felt sore and raw and she noticed there was blood on the wash cloth when she had taken her shower. Although she understood that it was Logan's first time too, common sense should have told him to take his time and be more gentle. The whole act had seemed so selfish on his part and she was repulsed . How in the world was she expected to live the rest of her life with this man? It was impossible.

Imari Rogan

Kashi was engrossed in her thoughts when she felt as though she was being watched. Then she smelled a familiar fragrance. She glanced up to see Reuben standing in front of her with a big smile on his face. "Hello Kashi," he said, with his deep and sexy voice. "Reuben!" she exclaimed. "It's so good to see you. You're a sight for sore eyes!" She wanted to jump up and tackle him to the ground but she restrained herself. He began to chuckle. "Oh really?" "Yes really!!" she sighed, as he took a seat on the bench beside her. As Reuben sat beside her, Kashi's mood changed and her eyes began to fill with tears. She didn't want to cry in front of him but right now she could really use a listening ear, even though they had just met. She felt as though he already knew her in a deep, meaningful way. She wanted to tell him everything that was bothering her as a friend who she knew would listen. Reuben looked at Kashi closely. "Is anything wrong?" His voice was full of concern. "Yes" she said slowly. "But it's a long story" "Well, I'm a good listener" He leaned in towards her to let her know that what she had to say was important to him.

She took a deep breath and began. "Well, I'm in a horrible predicament right now."

She paused for a moment before continuing. "Because of my ethnic background and traditional customs, I am being forced into an arranged marriage by my parents that was set up for me before I was even born. I've been dating my so called fiancé for about 2 years now and the problem is that I don't like him. The wedding is to take place after I turn 21 in June of next year. I argue constantly with my parents almost daily about the situation but they turn deaf ears to me. If I refuse to marry him, I am not breaking any laws but I may end up losing the respect of my parents and family. I don't want to be disowned, but I just can't imagine getting married to someone that I don't have any feelings for."

Reuben leaned back on the bench and took a deep breath before exhaling.

"That's torture." He responded. He looked so sympathetic. "Well how does your prospective fiancé feel about you?" "He adores me." Kashi said pitifully. "Reuben smiled "I can see why!!" They both started to laugh. "At least I got a smile out of you." he said "Yes but I'm miserable on the inside" "Well, I'm sorry that I don't have any answers for you. My background doesn't deal with those kind of issues although our problems are similar. While we don't have arranged marriages, we do deal with prejudice, sometimes in the worst way. But they are simply stipulations that we as humans and society place upon ourselves." "What do you mean? she asked. "Well for example, he continued, "When a black woman or man, such as myself, are interested or involved with anyone outside of our race, we are

44   Imari Rogan

sometimes automatically stereotyped and made fun of and pretty much ostracized by our families and friends. For the most part we just ignore it and move on." "You sound as if you are speaking from experience" she said.

Reuben paused for a long moment before he responded. "No" he said softly "But right now I wish that were my problem." He looked at her with a question in his eyes. She felt the heat rise in her cheeks. She was almost sure that her whole face had turned red. Was this his way of saying that he was interested? She didn't know how to respond. She looked at him with slight confusion. Without another word, he reached into his backpack and took out a pen and piece of paper. He scribbled his phone number on it and handed it to Kashi. "Let's keep in touch." Thank-you." she said softly. They stared at each other for a moment before a black Mercedes Benz with tinted windows pulled up to the curb. It was Logan. "That's my ride, I'd better go." Without another word she grabbed her belongings and ran to the car. Reuben managed to get slight a glimpse of the driver before the car pulled away. Kashi had offered no explanation as to who was picking her up. He watched the car as it slowly pulled away from the curb. He wondered if the driver of the Benz was Kashi's fiancé. He wondered if she would call him.

****

"Was that a black guy that you were talking to just now?" Logan angrily asked as they drove away. She thought back to the conversation that she and Reuben had just had. She chuckled before she answered. "Yes." "What's funny?" Logan didn't seem to be amused. Kashi didn't answer him. Logan continued. "As your future husband I think that I have the right to know who you were talking to especially of the opposite sex and black to be exact" She was furious. "Since when do you think that you own me?! She demanded. "And IF I decide to marry you, please keep in mind that you still won't own me!! Logan was startled at her response. He hadn't meant to sound so controlling but his emotions were running high right now. He some how felt threatened by this black man. Maybe it was the way he saw Kashi talking intently with him when he had driven up. "Look Kashi." he said lowering his voice. "It's just that when I saw you engrossed in conversation with him, I got a little jealous, please forgive me."

She glared at him and rolled her eyes. She stared out the window in silence. Logan knew that he had made her angry and decided that the best thing to do was keep silent. He finally asked her where she wanted to go and talk. "Some place

Imari Rogan

without distractions." She said. Logan knew just the place. There was a park that was only a few minutes away. This particular park was always secluded, it would be a perfect place for privacy.

Minutes later they pulled into the park and Logan found a parking place just near the lake's edge. It was practically deserted except for a jogger who ran by and disappeared among the trees. Logan cut the engine off, as Kashi leaned back into the heated leather bucket seats. They felt soothing and relaxing to her as she was starting to get a headache. She was enjoying the quiet but it was Logan who broke the silence. "What would you like to talk about?" He sounded anxious. At first he had been excited at the prospect of even just meeting with her, especially since she had initiated the meeting. Now he wasn't so sure anymore. He kind of thought that he had blown it and made matters worse by coming off as the jealous type, but something in him had just seemed to snap. He hoped that she had something positive to say but he didn't count on it.

Kashi massaged the sides of her temples with both hands for a moment before she quietly gave him the answer that he had been afraid to hear. She turned to face him and looked him straight in the eye. She spoke slowly and softly with an even tone. "Logan it's time for us to part company, I can't marry you. I have thought about it day and night. I have fought with myself, I have wrestled with my feelings and I have tried to make myself love you but after all is said and done I'm not in love with you. I just can't fake my feelings for you and it's not fair to either one of us. I just believe that marriage should be based on love and although you love me, I can't love you in return."

Logan looked as if his heart was breaking. "Kashi does this anything to do with the black guy that you were speaking with a few moments ago?" "No, Logan I don't even really know him that well, he's just someone that I met a few days ago at the bus stop who happens to attend the same university, but that's besides the point, I'm not in love with you Logan and I don't think that I'll ever be." Kashi's words slapped Logan in his face and he felt as if someone had just knocked the wind out of him. He felt as if someone had set off a time bomb in his heart. He turned away from her to look out of the window as he fought back tears. He didn't want her to see him cry. She touched him softly on the shoulder. "I'm sorry" she whispered. Logan turned to face her with tears streaming down his cheeks. He managed to speak but not without choking on his sobs. He felt as if he could hardly breathe. "Kashi this isn't right, this just isn't right, I love you so much, how could you do this to me? I feel so used." He said in between breaths. "Logan how can you say that? You pretend as if all of this is my fault, if you want to blame someone blame our parents, I have been talking to my parents for the past year telling them that I wanted out of our relationship, but they wouldn't hear of it. You're very perceptive and I'm sure you know that my feelings for you are not mutual, admit it."

Logan dropped his head in sorrow. He knew it was true. Kashi had always been distant and aloof but he had never wanted to accept those facts. He had been in denial and still was. "Kashi I thought that somehow over time that your feelings towards me would change, our parents are going to lose respect for us if we break up." "Well" she sighed, "That's too bad, I refuse to make us both miserable for God knows how long for the sake of our parents happiness, it's not worth it to me." "Kashi let me ask you a question," she nodded. "Why did you allow me to have sex with you?" She looked at Logan for a long moment before she answered. "To be honest Logan I thought that sex would make our relationship better, I thought it would change my feelings for you. I thought that it would make me love you but nothing changed. I'm really sorry Logan." Now it was Kashi's turn to feel sad. "Well, okay than." He replied. I guess that's it, when and how do we break the news to our parents?" he asked. Kashi thought for a long moment. "Why don't we not tell them anything for a while, like maybe a month or so, only because I don't feel like dealing with the arguments anytime soon." "Well what about our Friday night dates, how will we explain that?"

"I don't know but I'll think of something." "Okay" was all that Logan could manage to say. He wiped his tears away with the back of his hands. He felt stupid. He felt nauseated and dizzy. His world had come to a shattering end. There was nothing left to say. He silently started the car and they drove off in the direction of Kashi's home. It was now his turn to ignore Kashi and when she stepped out of the car and said goodbye, Logan ignored her. He stared straight ahead. She closed the door and headed towards the front entrance of the condo. Logan slowly drove away not even bothering to look to see if she had made it inside. He didn't know where he was going. He had no place to go. His entire world had shifted. He felt like dying.

He pulled back onto the main road that led back to the park. He returned to the empty parking lot, put the car in park, turned off the engine and sat quietly for a moment before suddenly opening the car door. The wave of nausea had hit him like a ton of bricks. He leaned out of the door and vomited. He threw up for what seemed like eternity. It seemed as though all of the sadness and disappointment that was within him came out. He wretched miserably until he was empty. He reached for a napkin from inside the glove box and wiped his mouth. His hands shook as he slammed the car door. Why me? He thought. Why did this have to happen to me? Sadness engulfed him as he drove home to his empty apartment and he fell across the bed sobbing. His sadness soon gave way to anger. There was no way that he was going to let this relationship be over. He simply wouldn't allow it to be. He refused to go out like a defeated washed up boxing opponent. Now it was time to fight!

6

As winter began to settle in, the state of Nebraska began to look like a winter wonderland. The snow covered ground and ice sickle covered trees made a beautiful sight to behold. Christmas was only two weeks away and it had been almost a month, since Kashi had broken up with Logan. The two had not spoken to each other since that horrible day in the park. Kashi was somewhat surprised that Logan hadn't attempted to call her. After all, the agreement had been to try and figure something out to tell their parents about why they were no longer dating, but under the circumstances, she just assumed that Logan was leaving everything up to her.

Thus far, she had been lying to her parents for the past few Fridays when asked why she wasn't going out by telling them that she was tired or not feeling well. Thankfully, they hadn't pressed the issue yet. She didn't know how long she could keep up the charade but for now, she had been enjoying her new found peace of mind. She was relieved emotionally and mentally to be away from Logan. Kashi and Reuben had talked numerous times, since he had given her his phone number and each time they had talked for hours. It was amazing how much they had in common. She found out they shared the same

Imari Rogan

interests when it came to books, movies and even sports. They both hated football but loved basketball and even liked the same foods....pizza, hot-dogs and tacos. A love for some of the same middle eastern foods was also something they shared.

They got to know each other really well over the next few weeks and had agreed to go out in the near future. She couldn't believe how much she was falling for him. When he finally asked her out a couple of weeks later, she happily said yes. The only dilemma would be where and when they would meet. Picking her up at home was totally out of the question and since her parents had just purchased a car for her, Kashi agreed it was best to meet someplace private, so they chose an evening after class, at the local coffee shop. Kashi was relieved she finally owned a car and would no longer need to depend on public transportation or Logan, for school or personal errands.

She arrived a few minutes early and waited in her car in the parking lot. Reuben arrived a few minutes later and parked in the space next to hers. He smiled, as he got out of his car and came around to help her out. He was definitely a gentlemen. She liked that. When their hands touched, it felt like electricity. They walked hand in hand into the dimly lit cafe, ordered their drinks and sat in a back corner booth. It was fairly empty at this time of day waiting for the evening rush. It was cozy and comfortable.

"It's good to see you again," Reuben said, smiling brightly. "Same here, how are things going?" "Okay, I guess but my dad is still kind of out there." Reuben had told Kashi all about his dad's affair. He hadn't planned on it but one night his father had come home late again and his mother was in tears. Reuben had no one to vent to, so he told Kashi all of the details. He knew that he could trust her and she had been very sympathetic and understanding regarding the situation. Although she didn't fully understand why his dad would do such things, Kashi tried nonetheless to sympathize with him. "Everything is going to be okay," Kashi whispered, as she reached across the table and brushed his hand. "Thanks," Reuben replied. They were silent for a moment before he asked her about Logan. "Well," she sighed, "I haven't heard from him since the breakup and quite frankly I'm glad, but I don't know how long it will be before my parents catch on, that we're not seeing each other." "Well, when they do, I'm sure it won't be easy for you but I'm always here for you." She looked into Reuben's eyes and knew that he meant it. Her heart skipped a beat. He always made her feel at ease...VERY at ease. Her feelings were starting to run deep and she hoped that he couldn't tell. Besides, it was way too early in their

Imari Rogan

relationship for her to even think about those types of feelings.

She tried to clear her head from the new emotions that began to well up inside of her. Their conversation was steady and easy and when they finally stopped talking, it was after dark. "Oh my gosh!! What time is it?" she asked. Rueben looked at his watch. "7:30," he replied. "7:30?, I didn't realize it was so late, I'd better get going." "Yeah, me too," he said standing up. He helped her from her seat and into her coat. "When will I see you again?' It was almost a whisper but Kashi heard him. She turned around and faced him and looked into his eyes. "Whenever you want." Their eyes locked for a long moment. She wanted to kiss him but didn't dare. "Okay, I'll call you soon," he managed to say. He could have stood there all night admiring her beauty and inhaling her intoxicating fruity scent but instead, he gently took her by the hand and led her to the parking lot. The fresh winter air had turned breezy and chilly. He walked her to her car and helped her inside. Kashi closed the door and rolled down the window. He leaned in and kissed her on the forehead. "See ya later," he said, as he walked to his car, got in and drove off. Kashi sat in the parking lot for a few minutes to get her emotions in check. She could still smell the faint fragrance of Reuben's cologne that lingered in the air. It was as intoxicating as he was. She was still trembling from the kiss he had placed on her forehead. His lips had felt warm and soft against her skin. She tried to imagine how his lips would feel against hers. As she sat in her car and continued to daydream, she suddenly began to feel uneasy. She didn't know why but she felt as if someone was watching her, within the shadows of the darkness. Kashi rolled up her window and quickly scanned the parking lot, in an attempt to verify her uneasiness. She watched as people were coming and going into the coffee shop but nothing looked out of the ordinary. Still, she felt as if someone was watching her. She nervously started the car and hurriedly pulled out of the parking lot, while keeping her eyes fixed on the rear view mirror. What was she running from? She convinced herself that she was being ridiculous. After spending a wonderful evening with Reuben, she wasn't about to let anything spook her now.

****

He watched them intently. More so her than him. But nonetheless he watched. He noticed that when she laughed, she kind of tilted her head back....almost mockingly. He noticed what she was wearing. He watched them as they walked out of the coffee

Imari Rogan

shop. *So carefree, happy and oblivious to their surroundings. He did what he had to do and in record time no doubt. He noticed after she had gotten settled into her car, that she began to look around. It was almost as if she knew that someone was watching her. It seemed as though she gazed in his direction and he quickly ducked behind his newspaper. Maybe she wasn't so dumb after all. He watched her slowly drive away, while nervously checking her rear view mirror. Maybe this task wouldn't be so easy after all.*

7

Christmas came quickly. The two week winter break from college had arrived and Kashi didn't know how she was going to spend her time. It had been a couple of weeks, since her last date with Reuben and she was anxious to see him again. Although they talked everyday on the phone, she longed to look into his deep brown eyes. She hoped that his plans for winter break included her but she didn't inquire . She didn't want to appear pushy because that was the quickest way to get rid of someone. Logan had taught her that firsthand.

She woke up late on Christmas morning to the sounds of laughter coming from the living room. She and Reuben had stayed up late talking on her cell phone the night before. It was almost 3 a.m. when they had finally said goodnight. He had wished her a Merry Christmas and told her that he would talk to her soon.

Kashi was still somewhat groggy as she stepped into the living room, where the twins were giggling and opening up gifts. "Merry Christmas," said her mother, smiling from ear to ear. "Merry Christmas mom," Kashi said, while giving her mother a long hug....something she didn't do very often. She buried her head on her mother's shoulder and inhaled the fragrance of her freshly shampooed hair. Kashi's mother lovingly stroked her hair. It was times like this that she wished that her mother would never let her go. She felt so safe and secure in her arms. She wished her mother would understand. They finally made eye contact and her mom asked her if everything was okay. She was so tempted to tell her that she had broken up with Logan and was now seeing someone else. She really wanted her mother's approval but thought better of it. "Everything's fine mom, where's dad?" she asked, looking over her shoulder towards the empty dining room. "He had to go to the hospital to deliver Ms. Johnson's baby. She went into labor early this morning and insisted that your father do the delivery." " I see, well ".......she sighed, "Open up the gift that I bought for you and dad" Her mom's eyes lit up, as she rushed towards the Christmas tree. She hurriedly found the giant box signed from Kashi and opened it with excitement. It contained the blue ray disc player that she knew her mom and dad had talked about. Kashi's mom threw her arms around Kashi again. 'Thank-you," she squealed "Do you like it?" "I love it and so will your father" "Open ours, open ours," squealed the twins, while yanking on Kashi's arm. "Okay, okay," as Kashi reached under the tree and retrieved the twins' gifts. They had each given her a Victoria's Secret body lotion and perfume set and a night shirt. "Thank you," she said giving them each a big hug and kiss, which Jason promptly wiped off. She was enjoying the moment when she was distracted by the house phone. "I'll get it" she said, as she went into the kitchen to answer the phone.

"Hello, Merry Christmas," she sang into the phone. She heard a long silence and then the caller hung up. That was strange, Kashi thought, as she glanced at the caller ID. The phone number had been blocked. She returned to the living room when the phone rang again. Somewhat annoyed, she returned to the kitchen, glanced at the caller ID and realized the number was blocked again but she answered anyway. "Hello is anyone there?" Another long silence and then, "I hope you're having a Merry Christmas," from the caller, who sounded very sarcastic. At first, Kashi thought the caller had the wrong number when she suddenly recognized the voice. It was Logan.

"Yes," she answered "As a matter of a fact, I am having a Merry Christmas and you?" "Well, It would be better If you were here to spend it with me," he said sarcastically. She didn't like the tone of Logan's voice. He had never sounded like this before. He sounded......dangerous. "Look Logan" she said very slowly. She tried to keep her voice calm but he had already unnerved her. "I'm glad that you called me to wish me a Merry Christmas. Now is there anything else I can help you with?" "Yes!"

he almost yelled "As a matter of a fact there is. As a special Christmas gift to you, I'm going to tell your parents you dumped me and I'm doing that today!" he shouted. Oh God! Kashi thought. Not now. Not today. Her stomach began to unsettle and her hands started to tremble. She thought of what she would say next but before she could protest, he hung up.

She stood in the kitchen for a few more minutes, with the receiver still in her hand and tried to regain her composure. Logan had never spoken to her that way and he sounded like a deranged madman. She was afraid. She had never really seen Logan lose his temper until now. She knew that eventually her parents would find out about the breakup but she didn't want them to find out today, not like this. Not on Christmas and especially when Logan was this angry. She decided not to let it go. She called Logan back. "Yes?" was all he said, when he answered the phone. "Logan look, I don't want you to tell my parents that we broke up. At least not yet and not today." "Oh really?" he said, in a mocking tone" "No, really!" Kashi was almost breathless as she spoke and Logan began to laugh a deep throaty and sinister laugh. He laughed so hard that he started to cough.

Kashi was spooked...really spooked. When he finally gathered himself, he began to speak. "Okay Kashi, I'll make a deal with you. We're still officially broken up but to make things look good for me on my end and to look good for you on your end, we'll fake it. We'll each have dinner at both of our parents' homes like we do every Christmas. Is that understood?" Kashi couldn't believe what she was hearing but at the same time it sounded like a reasonable remedy given the situation. She hadn't even thought about the possibility of what her parents would think, when they didn't spend Christmas together until now. "Yes Logan, I understand but how long will we keep up this charade? I feel as if I'm being blackmailed." "We will keep up the charade until you get the nerve to tell our parents that you dumped me."

Kashi was furious but she was too afraid to disagree. "Okay then," she obliged "What time is dinner?" "I'll pick you up at 3:00, we'll eat at my parent's home and then return to your house around 7:00, as we've always done in the past. It's a tradition."

Before she had a chance to respond, he hung up. "Kashi," called her mother from the living room. Who was that on the phone?" "Logan," she responded "Are you having the usual dinner at his house today?" "Yes mom," she responded from the kitchen. She quickly rushed to her bedroom before her mother could ask any more questions. Kashi sat down on the bed in a huff. The only good thing about the situation is that it gave her more time before telling her parents about the breakup. That part she didn't mind so much, but she was furious that Logan would try to blackmail her. She hated him now more than ever. She didn't know what kind of game he was playing but she didn't want to play it with him. Kashi had a feeling that her two week vacation was going to be hell.

****

Logan arrived at Kashi's place promptly at 3:00. He was wearing a slick smile on his face that told Kashi he was serious about their earlier conversation. "Hello Mr. and Mrs. Pattel!" he exclaimed, when he stepped into the living room. "Hello Logan, it's good to see you and Merry Christmas." Her father beamed with joy, while standing to shake Logan's hand. Kashi's mother rushed to give him a bear hug. After the pleasantries, Logan asked Kashi if she was ready? "Ready," Kashi said, while giving a huge fake smile to throw her parents off. They were smiling so approvingly in the background. "See you at 7:00" Kashi called out, as she closed the door behind them.

Once outside, Logan forcefully grabbed her under the arm and escorted her to the car. He was hurting her. "Ouch," she shrieked, while trying to pull away. He had never treated her like this but she knew he was still angry about the break up. Luckily, after Logan helped Kashi into the car, his mood began to soften. "I'm sorry Kashi, It's just that I love you so much," he said, with his voice breaking. She looked over at him and saw his eyes were glassy. "Logan, let's just try to get through the evening okay?" she said softly. "Okay" he whispered, while taking her hand in his. She wanted to pull away but didn't dare. The odds were against her right now and she didn't want to facilitate his anger any further. She forced herself to play along. He made light conversation with her as they drove to his parent's mansion. Kashi pretended to show interest in what Logan was saying but her mind was a million miles away.

****

Dinner was delicious. Logan's mother was a great cook. The food was the only thing the entire evening that Kashi had enjoyed. Logan had sat shoulder to shoulder with her at the table, taking pleasure in her obvious discomfort. She could tell he was taking full advantage of every moment. Logan was making jokes at Kashi's expense and teasing her in front of his family. She wasn't good at being fake but she tried her best. She pasted on a fake smile and tried to laugh her way through dinner but it was almost pointless. The one question she dreaded hearing all evening finally came. The question that she hoped would not be mentioned tonight. In the middle of dessert, Logan's father asked Kashi how the wedding plans were going. Logan nudged her saying, "Yes how are the plans coming?" Kashi nearly choked on her Gulab Jamun, a popular Indian pastry.

She took a large sip of water before answering. She saw Logan out of the corner of her eye waiting anxiously to hear her response. "Fine," she said rather too quickly. "Just fine." "Is your dress already picked out?" asked his mom. "Yes, Mrs. Roy, it's beautiful." She wasn't lying about that. The dress was beautiful and she had no intentions of returning it to the store. She would wear it someday to marry the person that she really loved. "When can I see it?" asked Logan, somewhat mockingly. "On our wedding day," she replied sweetly, without even looking at him. How she hated him with every passing minute. He was doing this on purpose!! Kashi started eating her danish again and pretended to be engrossed in it. She hoped that the "wedding" conversation was over. She needed to talk to someone, who would understand everything she was going through and knew her true feelings.

"Excuse me please," she said, on the verge of tears. Kashi excused herself from the table and began walking down the hall. Logan started to go after her but she turned and gave him a look that told him to back off. She hurriedly walked to the powder room and quietly closed the door behind her. Hot tears of frustration began to stream down her cheeks. How had she gotten herself into this situation? She closed the lid and sat down on the edge of the toilet. She rummaged through her purse until she found her cell phone and dialed Reuben's number. He answered on the second ring.

"Hello?" he said cheerfully. Just hearing his voice made her cry. She could barely say hello through her tears. "Kashi, what's wrong?" Once she caught her breath, she explained the whole ordeal to Reuben and told him she was hiding out in the bathroom. "Don't worry Kashi, everything is going to be fine. Would you like to get together tonight, so we can talk? It may make you feel better" That was an answer to her prayers. "Yes, I would love to see you but we have to go back to my mom and dad's after this for a little while. It may be late when everything is finally over." "That's okay, I have all the time in the world for you." Her heart skipped a beat. In the corner of her mind, Kashi imagined Reuben holding her. "Okay, I'll tell you what...after we meet with my parents and Logan leaves, I'll make up an excuse to go out and we can meet somewhere." "Okay that sounds good but not too many places will be open on Christmas night." "That's right!" Kashi was silent for a moment, while they both thought. "How about the Holiday Inn hotel lobby? They have a fireplace and a sitting area," Reuben suggested. "Okay that sounds good. I'll call you when I'm on my way." A knock on the bathroom door interrupted their conversation. From outside the door, Logan asked Kashi if she was okay.

"I'll see you later Reuben, I have to go," she whispered into the phone before hanging up. Kashi slipped her phone back into her purse and wondered how long he had been standing there. "I'm fine" she answered "I'll be right out." She flushed the toilet and turned on the water to make her bathroom visit sound legitimate. She checked her make-up and stepped out into the hallway, looking as if she didn't have a care in the world. Logan clearly glared at her before escorting her back to the kitchen.

The dishes had already been cleared and his family was heading to the family room. Logan followed too closely behind her. Everyone chatted for a few minutes before Kashi announced they had better return to her parent's house. She kissed Logan's parents goodbye with promises that she would see them soon. She really did adore his parents. They were nice people. She would not have minded one bit to have them as in-laws. It was their son that she hated. She knew they would be hurt and angry after all of this was over but it was a chance she was willing to take. She wasn't going to ruin her life with their son.

Logan drove way too slowly on the drive back home. It seemed as if he was driving under the speed limit. Logan was purposely trying to aggravate Kashi just because he could. As soon as they walked through the front entrance of the condo, her parents were all over Logan. They were always complimenting him and saying how proud they were of him, and how lucky Kashi was to have him. Kashi wanted to puke. She knew better. After the praise party ended, they all sat down in the family room and her father popped a movie into his new blu-ray player. Unfortunately, it was a cushy love story. Just what Logan wanted to see. He pulled Kashi close and dared her, with his eyes, to protest. She squirmed within his embrace but he ignored her. How she wished he'd fall over dead. To get through the evening, Kashi imagined that the two lovers in the movie were her and Reuben. Her mood changed for the better. She actually let herself relax in Logan's embrace.

"Feeling better?" he whispered in her ear, while tightening his grip. She looked up at him through squinted eyes but said nothing. When the movie finally ended she lied, said she was tired and needed to go to bed. Logan was fresh out of excuses to keep her occupied any longer. It was time to go home. Besides, he was scheduled to work in the morning. He reluctantly stood to his feet and said his goodbyes. Kashi walked him to the door. He kissed her on the cheek. She closed the door behind him and wiped his kiss from her face, which now felt dirty. She said goodnight to her parents and excused herself to her bedroom. She was exhausted from the long day but she freshened up and changed her clothes. Excited about meeting Rueben, she looked at her watch. It was 10:30. It seemed as though she waited an eternity before she finally heard her parent's door close. She quietly tiptoed down the hall and made it outside to her car, where she called Reuben. "Ready?" she asked, when he answered. "Ready. I'll see you in 20 minutes." Kashi could hardly wait. She checked her makeup in the rear view mirror and sprayed on the new perfume she had gotten for Christmas. She drove the short ride to the hotel in sweet anticipation of seeing Reuben again. When she arrived, Reuben was already seated waiting for her in the lobby. He looked up when he saw her come in and stood to greet her. She was so beautiful and radiant in her pair of slim fitting black jeans, red turtleneck sweater and black shearling jacket. The black lambskin leather riding boots were form fitting on her calves. What a classy lady he thought to himself. They embraced lightly before sitting down.

"You look just like a fashion model" Kashi blushed, but she hardly thought so. "So how did things go?" Reuben asked. "Just Horrible. I had to fake being polite all evening and pretend that nothing was wrong just to impress our parents. How long can I keep this up?" "Well, sooner or later, your parents are going to find out, since your wedding is only about nine months away." She hadn't realized until that moment how soon the time had snuck up on her. She buried her head in her hands. "Hey, we'll think of something...... together, Reuben said. "You would do that for me? I mean you don't even really know me." "Says who?" he asked, as he placed his hand on the side of her neck. He began to massage the tension away. "Hmmmmm," Kashi moaned. That felt so good. The tension began to melt. Reuben's hands worked their magic on her tired and tense neck muscles. She wanted him to touch her in other places, but thought better of it. "Thanks, I feel better now" she said, indicating that he should stop. She was afraid that if he didn't, they'd end up in one of the rooms upstairs.

"I have an idea" he said, breaking the awkwardness of the moment. Kashi turned to face him, listening intently. "Since Logan has left all of the responsibility of the break up in your lap and he wants you to be the one to tell everyone it was your decision to breakup, then why don't you just tell everyone, including Logan, you need more time to think. In other words, he continued, seeing her look of confusion, just postpone the wedding temporarily, telling everyone that you want to wait a little while just to get yourself together. Tell them that you want your marriage to Logan to be perfect and that your feelings need to be legitimate. Tell them that you're working on your emotions and postpone the wedding. That way no one will think that it's totally over and it will buy you all the time that you need to throw them off. By doing it that way, you don't have to worry about making up excuses for Friday night dates and so forth. BUT in the meantime, Logan will probably get tired of waiting for you and totally break it off with you."

She thought for a long moment before responding. "So what you're suggesting is that I inform Logan and our families that the wedding is only being postponed, opposed to calling it off. That way Logan can stop harassing me if he thinks that there is still hope but if I postpone it long enough, he may get impatient and call it off altogether?" Reuben was smiling and slowly nodding his head in agreement. Kashi thought that the idea was brilliant. A postponement would throw everyone off but keep everyone satisfied at the same time. She was so overcome with relief that she pulled Reuben into her arms and hugged him without realizing it. Reuben was an awesome friend. They continued to talk until 3:00 am. "Oh my God! It's 3am! she exclaimed, as she jumped up off the couch. I have to get home!" "I'm sorry I kept you so late," Reuben responded. "Don't be, it was well worth it." Reuben stared into Kashi's eyes and felt the heat rise to his chest. He couldn't help himself any longer. He tilted her chin upwards toward his and slowly kissed her lips with one soft kiss. When she didn't resist, he kissed her again. This time with a tad more passion. Their lips melted into one another's if only for a brief moment. It was Reuben, who pulled away first. Kashi stared at him in awe. "Let me walk you to your car." They held hands and walked silently. He promised that he would call her soon before he watched her drive away. The smell of his cologne lingered on her jacket and she thought about never taking it off. He was turning out to be more than a friend and as she drove home, she imagined what life would be like with Reuben.

****

The black guy must have thought that a rain storm was coming by the way he twirled around after the flash went off. He gazed towards the sky. How stupid could he be?! He had watched them the entire time. Inside of the hotel lobby and finally outside. The Indian girl was a hot number. He was positive that any man would be glad to drown her in kisses the way that the black guy had done. He didn't blame him. He was one lucky son of a bitch. Personally speaking, he didn't have anyone that would meet him at home tonight. He was going home to a couple of old movies on TV and settle in with a hot bowl of soup. How exciting but that was besides the point. He had a job to do and he was going to do it. He was going to be so very proud of his work, when all of this was over.

8

During Christmas vacation, Kashi and Reuben continued to talk on the phone and they went to the movies twice. Kashi could only dream of the day when they could go out as a couple in the same vehicle and not have to sneak to meet each other. But she knew that her parents would never accept her dating anyone else other than Logan. She waited until New Year's Eve to tell everyone about postponing the wedding, including Logan. Kashi's parents threw a New Year's Eve gala at the condo that night and several couples came out. Logan had shown up with his parents. The evening was festive and lively and Kashi was actually enjoying herself.

Everyone was talking and laughing, while seated around the fireplace, when Kashi beckoned for Logan to come with her. His eyes lit up like the Christmas tree in the corner, as he followed her down the hall. Once inside the den, Kashi closed the door for privacy. "We have to talk," she said, when they were alone. Kashi took a seat on the sofa and Logan sat opposite of her on the love seat. "Yes, what's going on?" Logan asked. She took a deep breath before she answered. "Logan, I've been doing a great deal of thinking."

She paused before she continued. "Would it be okay with you if we just postponed the wedding for a while instead of just breaking up altogether? I need a little more time to think." Logan looked surprised. "Think about what?" he asked, somewhat irritated. "Why the change of heart all of a sudden?" He looked at her suspiciously. She nervously continued.

"Well I know that marriage is a big step and I'm not opposed to it, but right now I just need a little more time to sort things out. I want us to be happy as a couple and I especially want you to be happy and I want to be the perfect wife but right now my frame of mind is not ready to take on that kind of responsibility".

She waited for his response. What if he disagreed? He seemed to be processing what she had asked him. "How long are you asking that we postpone things?" he asked. She let out a long sigh. "Maybe until next year this time and if you really love me Logan, I think you should be willing to wait."

She watched as his whole demeanor changed. He went from suspicious to vulnerable. "Kashi I love you more than anything on this earth and if you need a little more time to sort things out then so be it. Take all of the time that you need. I want everything to be right between us but I need to ask you a question" Kashi braced herself. "Sure," she answered. "Does this have anything to do with Reuben?" A silent icy fear washed over Kashi. She wasn't sure but she didn't remember ever mentioning Reuben's name to Logan. How did he know his name? A silent tremor went down her spine. Had he been listening to her conversation on Christmas night, while she talked on her cell phone in the bathroom? How could this be? He must have been standing outside of the door listening to her talk. She had only told Logan once that Reuben was a friend and that was the day he had picked her up from school. And even then, she had not mentioned his name. She reasoned that he had overheard her conversation. "No," she finally answered. "It has nothing to do with him and how do you know his name?" He stared at her with an icy silence, as if he knew something that she didn't. When he still didn't answer, she continued. "It has nothing to do with him but I just need more time." He leaned forward and studied her expression very carefully. "Okay" he said, sounding convinced.

"When do you think we should break the news to our families?" "Let's wait until after the New Year," Kashi suggested. He nodded his head in agreement. "I'll tell mine and you tell yours?" she suggested. "Okay, I think I can live with that Kashi Pattel," he smiled. "Okay, Logan Roy" Kashi said, smiling back.

She stood to her feet and placed a light kiss on Logan's cheek. Logan pulled her close to him and this time she didn't pull away. He hugged her

Imari Rogan

for a long time and she allowed it. She had to stall him long enough to make him think they were really getting married. Just play along, she told herself. This plan may just work after all, she thought to herself. Thanks to Reuben.

The clock struck midnight and the guests toasted the New Year in with raised champagne glasses. The kids threw confetti into the air and couples kissed on cue. As Kashi looked around the room, she silently wished that Reuben was there to kiss her. She glanced across the opposite end of the room and looked at Logan. He met her gaze and nodded his head in her direction. With a raised champagne glass, Kashi nodded back and took a sip from her flute. No one seemed to notice that Kashi and Logan were the only couple in the room, who were not embraced. Logan looked sad and dejected and Kashi felt a bit sorry for him. She felt sorry for herself too because now more than ever she wished that she was in Reuben's arms.

9

New Year's day found Kashi and her family winding down from the festivities and getting ready for their upcoming New Year schedules. It would be back to work and school as usual. Kashi had gotten spoiled over Christmas vacation and dreaded going back to classes but she knew that would give her more opportunity to bump into Reuben on campus. Kashi was dozing in her bedroom, when she was awakened by the ringing phone in the distance. She turned over and pulled the covers over her head. As she tried to go back to sleep, she was interrupted by a loud knock on her bedroom door. "Yes?" she answered sleepily. "Kashi, we need to talk" It was her father's voice on the other side of the door. He sounded really upset. Now what? she thought. "Just a minute. I'll be right out"

She went into her bathroom, brushed her teeth and splashed cold water on her face. She slipped into her robe and house shoes and padded down the hallway into the living room, where both her parents sat quietly waiting. "Take a seat," her father demanded, pointing towards the couch. She did as she was told. From the tone of her father's voice, it was serious. When she was seated, her father asked about the break up between her and Logan. "What?" asked Kashi.

She wanted her father to explain what she thought he may already know. "Logan's father just called a moment ago to inform us that the wedding was postponed. Is this true?" "Yes dad, but only for a little while. I was going to tell the both of you in a few days and Logan was supposed to wait and tell his parents in a few days as well, but I guess he changed his mind." "How long of a postponement and why?" asked her father. "At least a year" "A YEAR?!!!" yelled her father. Kashi remained silent for a moment. "Yes dad, a year and it was my decision."

She noticed her father getting more angry but she held up her hand in protest before she continued. "You want me to be happy with the decision that you made for me to marry Logan and I need for the both of us to be happy and if that is ever going to be, then I need more time to get myself together and try to fall in love with him. I need to get my emotions in check and for that to happen, I simply won't be ready by June." Kashi's father looked at her mother and then back at Kashi. He didn't seem to agree with what he was hearing. "You need to explain to me what is going on?" "I just did! I have pleaded with both of you," she said, quickly glancing at her mother "and you have both been very unreasonable and biased about the way that I feel. So to make everyone happy, I decided that I need a little more time. You want me to be happy with a decision that YOU made for me and if that's going to be, then everyone should be able to respect my wishes and give me more time. When I do marry Logan, everyone including myself should be happy." Kashi's mom dropped her head and stared at the floor, too embarrassed to say anything. Her father looked completely disgusted. "Okay" he finally sighed. "But I'm warning you not to make Logan wait too long. He has too much to offer you and you don't want to push him away" And that was exactly what she wanted. She stifled the urge to laugh. "And if he loves me he will wait, and if I am to love him, everyone involved will wait." The fire had returned to Kashi's eyes as she spoke. She knew that her parents had no choice but to comply. "I will make sure that the caterers know the wedding is postponed until next Christmas," her mother said standing. Kashi's father nodded his head in agreement and left the room. So much for that. Kashi wanted to scream a victory scream but resisted. She felt victorious. The biggest challenge was now over. Now all she had to do was wait for Logan to get tired of waiting for her and dump her.

New Year's day at Reuben's home was anything but festive. His father had stayed out all night long and had returned home this morning drunk and hungover. He had stumbled through the door at 6:00 a.m. and didn't care who that bothered. His mother was sitting at the kitchen table reading the newspaper and drinking coffee when he staggered in. They started to argue and the fight had awakened Reuben. He went downstairs to the kitchen to see what the argument was about. His father was screaming and yelling at his mother shouting that he could come home whenever he wanted. His mother was standing in his father's face yelling that she had to spend New Year's Eve all by herself and that she knew all about Tina. Reuben didn't know whether to walk back out of the kitchen or remain. He was shocked. He wondered how his mother had found out about the affair. Reuben's father looked angrily in his direction and approached him with fire in his eyes. His father then knocked him in the face with his fist and Reuben fell to the floor.

"Did you tell her?!, Did you tell her?!" his father screamed, as he stood over him in a rage. His breath reeked of alcohol. Reuben hadn't told his mom anything about Tina. He wondered himself how she knew? He struggled to stand on his feet but he was too dizzy from the head blow. His mom screamed for his dad to leave him alone.

"It's not his fault, it's not his fault" his mom pleaded. "Leave him alone. I found out on my own!!" His father turned to his wife and slapped her across the face, with an open hand. Reuben watched in horror, as his mother lost her balance. She fell to the floor but not before hitting her head on the side of the kitchen table.

Reuben managed to stand to his feet and lunged at his father from behind. As he managed to get both of his hands around his father's neck, he began to choke him for dear life. He wanted him to die but he was no match for his father. His father managed to break out of his grip and the fight ensued. They punched and swung at each other, knocking over kitchen chairs, while dishes fell from the table to the floor.

Reuben stumbled over his mother, who was still sprawled out on the floor. She appeared to be unconscious. Reuben swung again at his father punching him hard in his eye, and across the top of his head. His father fell to the floor in a daze and this time he didn't get up. He lay on the floor breathless and bleeding. The entire room looked as if a tornado had swept through. There was blood splattered in various places in the kitchen and dishes and broken glass lay strewn about the floor.

Reuben stood over his father glaring at him with hatred. "If you ever touch my mother again, I'll kill you! he sneered. Reuben then moved to his mother's side and knelt on the floor beside her. She wasn't moving. He gently shook her shoulder. "Mom! Mom!" but she didn't respond.

Imari Rogan

Reuben grabbed his cell phone and dialed 911. "911 what's your emergency?

"Hello, there was a domestic dispute between my parents and my mom has fallen and hit her head. She's unconscious."

"Is she breathing? asked the operator. "I'm not sure" he whimpered. "Please send an ambulance right away" Reuben gave the operator his address and hung up.

He gathered his mother's unresponsive body into his arms. He cried as he rocked her back and forth. "Please be okay, please be okay" he cried. Reuben's father stumbled to his feet and staggered past them as if nothing happened. Reuben cried in silence and prayed that his mom would be okay. He heard the sirens in the distance and left his mom's side to open the door. Everything was a blur as the technicians asked questions, took vitals and finally placed his mom in the back of the ambulance. Reuben rode along with them, while the paramedics worked feverishly administering oxygen, monitoring vitals and checking her blood pressure.

When they arrived at the hospital, his mother had still not regained consciousness. God please don't let her die he begged. They immediately rushed her to one of the rooms in the ER and began working on her. One of the nurses told Reuben to wait in the waiting room but he didn't want to leave his mother's side. It was the

ER doctor who finally convinced him it would be best to wait in the waiting room. Reuben took a seat in the corner of the room. He dropped his head into his hands and wept uncontrollably. His cell phone vibrated in his pocket. It was Kashi. He could barely say hello. His voice was almost a whisper. Kashi immediately knew something was wrong, as soon as she heard him. "Reuben what is it, what's wrong?" He managed to explain to her what had just taken place. "I'll be right there!" he heard Kashi say, before the phone disconnected. He didn't want her to see him this way but he really needed his friend right now.

He was still crying when she arrived. She rushed to his side and he reached out to hug her. He allowed her to hold him, while he cried. His mom was his world and his everything. He couldn't face the fear of losing her. After a long moment, a doctor approached them. "Mr. Griffin?" he asked looking directly at Reuben. "Yes" Reuben responded, standing up to greet the doctor. "I'm Dr. Robbins, the attending ER physician and I've been working on your mom. May I have a word alone with you?" he asked, giving Kashi a glance. "Of course doctor" They moved to a secluded side of the waiting room and Dr. Robbins began to explain his mother's situation. His mother had suffered major head trauma from the fall she had taken. The cat scan wasn't clear at the time of whether or not his mother's brain was bruised or actually bleeding. But it was clear that she was in a coma and they would have to wait for the swelling in her brain to diminish before making any major decisions. As of now, his mother had been transferred to ICU and he could see her for a few moments. In the meantime, everything else would be touch and go. Reuben felt his knees buckle and Dr. Robbins caught him before he hit the floor. Kashi had been observing the conversation from the other side of the room and rushed over to assist the doctor with Reuben. They helped him take a seat and Kashi gave him a sip from her water bottle. "Are you okay?" the doctor asked. "Yes, I'll be fine, just a little upset right now." He paused for a moment to gather himself. "Can I go and see my mom now?" "Yes you may" answered the doctor. "Can my girlfriend come with me?" Reuben asked looking directly at Kashi. Their eyes locked for a brief moment. "Of course," said Dr. Robbins, who led them down the hall to the ICU unit.

Once inside the room, Reuben walked over to his mother's bedside with Kashi beside him. There was a tube inserted in her throat and her head was wrapped in bandages. Both arms had IV needles and the sounds of the heart monitor and respirator were almost too much for Reuben to bear. He leaned over the railing of his mother's bedside and let the tears fall once again. His father had almost killed his mom. What an ungrateful bastard his dad was. To have such a beautiful treasure as this and willingly mess it up. Kashi pulled Reuben into her arms and let him cry. "It's going to be okay" she whispered, as she rubbed and stroked his back. "Everything is going to be okay," she assured him. Once again, Reuben felt safe and comfortable in Kashi's embrace. He prayed that her words of reassurance were correct.

10

It didn't take long for Reuben to realize that something was wrong: things seemed kind of amiss. He had noticed it the moment he was helping his mom into the car. His mother had made a drastic improvement physically and now two weeks later they were releasing her from the hospital. It had been a touch and go situation at first and Reuben was on standby to kill his father. After each visit to the hospital, Reuben would return home to the same old questions from his father asking how she was doing. Not once did his father set foot in the hospital to check on his wife. The selfish asshole that he was, refused to take any responsibility for what he had done. Instead, he blamed his mom for her own fall. Reuben's brother and sister were furious with their dad and when his brother found out what happened, he promptly went over to the house, punched his dad in his nose and broke it. His brother threatened to kill him if he ever touched their mother again. Reuben also enlightened his siblings about the affair between their father and Tina. They were both livid. Everyone had agreed their mother would recuperate at home and afterwards would try to convince her to leave their father.

When his mother was finally settled into the car, Reuben closed the door and noticed something that really stood out. There was a long deep scratch that had taken some of the paint off of the exterior. Obviously someone had keyed his car door and it looked very fresh. He was sure it wasn't there when he arrived at the hospital. He would have noticed it. Who would do something like this? He had no enemies to speak of except his father but it would be ludicrous for his dad to do something like that. Now he would have to shell out extra cash to repair the damages. He was disgusted but had no time to dwell on it at the moment. Right now his main focus was his mom. He climbed into the driver's side. "Ready to go?" he asked "Ready!" said his mom with a big smile. As he drove away, his phone rang. The number was unknown but he answered anyway. "Hello?"

No response but he could hear someone breathing. "Hello!" he said again. Click. He angrily placed his cell on the dashboard. "Who was that?" his mom asked. "Prank caller I guess." But he was somewhat unnerved. First the scratch on his car and now the weird phone call. What was going on? Not many people had his cell phone number except for close friends and family. On the way home, Reuben tried to convince himself that it was only a prank call and there was nothing to worry about but somehow, he wasn't convinced .

****

Imari Rogan

The rest of the day was beautiful and uneventful. The sun was bright and the snow was starting to melt a little. Kashi decided to do some shopping at the mall and she took the twins with her for company. Reuben would be picking his mom up from the hospital today and she was going to give him some space. She admired the way he stood by his mother's side during her illness. It had been a rough ride but somehow his mother had made it through. Kashi had been very supportive of Reuben during the ordeal, always making sure that she was available whenever he needed to talk or visit. She made Reuben a priority. She had met him several times at the hospital and they had talked for hours. She remembered how he had referred to her as his "girlfriend" the first day that his mother was admitted. She smiled as she thought about it. She guessed that she really was his "girlfriend". No other words about it had been spoken since then but it was obvious they were in a real "relationship".

She had not heard from Logan since New Year's day and she was happy. Kashi refocused her attention on her shopping expedition. Jessica and Jason were having a great time at the mall, dodging in and out of their favorite stores and eating junk food all day. Kashi silently prayed they wouldn't be sick in the middle of the night but it would be her fault if they did. She just couldn't resist spoiling them. It was almost dark when they finally left the mall. The parking lot was somewhat empty as they made their way to the car. Their arms were loaded with shopping bags, as they dumped them into the trunk. Kashi let the twins in and made her way to her side of the car. That was when she noticed that something was wrong.

The car was sort of leaning to one side on the driver's side. Kashi stooped down to see what was wrong. Great!! A flat tire. But it didn't appear to be an ordinary flat tire. It appeared that that the tire was somewhat mangled. As she peered a little closer, she saw a deep slash on the side of it. It looked as though someone had taken a large knife of some type and slashed her tire. She let out an angry sigh, got into the car, and slammed the door. "What's wrong?" Jessica asked. "We have a flat tire." "How will we get home?" asked Jason. "Don't worry about it!!" she snapped. Feeling irritated, she looked through the contacts in her phone until she found the 24 hour road service number. She dialed it and informed the operator of her situation and her location. She was told a tow truck would be there within a half hour but the three of them anxiously waited for over an hour, before the truck finally arrived. The mechanic changed the tire and replaced it with her spare tire from the trunk. "Ma'am this looks deliberate. Do you have

Imari Rogan

any enemies?" asked the tow driver, when he finished replacing the tire. "None that I can think of, why do you ask?" "Well," he continued "as I said, it appears as if someone did this on purpose." Kashi shivered against the cold evening air and tried to reassure herself that no one would do such a thing. He wrote her receipt, handed it to her and told her to be safe before driving away. Kashi was scared. Enemies? She didn't have any enemies. She didn't deny that someone had slashed her tires but he must have chosen the wrong vehicle. Enemies? RIDICULOUS!!

Later that evening, Kashi called Reuben to see how his mom was doing. He told her of the prognosis and said she was comfortably settled in. Reuben also mentioned that his sister had taken a short leave of absence from her job to take care of their mom, while he finished his classes. His father had temporarily moved into a hotel where he would feel more comfortable. He didn't need to be under the same roof with two angry children and a wife, who cared less about his feelings right now. Kashi asked if there was anything she could do. "As a matter of a fact there is. Do you think that you could stop by for a little while because I could really use a hug." She blushed as she felt the butterflies began to dance in her stomach. It was getting late and she didn't want to drive on the temporary spare tire but she didn't want to disappoint Reuben either. Besides, she could use a hug too. She had never been to Reuben's home before but she was somewhat familiar with the area. She remembered the day they had taken the bus together from class and his stop had been the first one. She remembered where his subdivision was located.

With the address in hand, she arrived at the sub and her mouth gaped open, as she drove past the massive and elaborate homes. They were simply breathtaking. She pulled into the circular driveway and parked behind Reuben's car. She walked what seemed like a half mile from the driveway to the front entrance. She glanced upwards at the huge diamond like chandelier that glowed in the arch shaped window above the double entry doors. She could see the winding staircase from the outside window, as she peered in and rang the bell. She noticed a striking, beautiful young woman descend down the stairs and come towards the door. The door opened and the woman greeted Kashi with a huge smile. "Hello, you must be Kashi, I'm Reuben's sister Ariel," she said, extending her hand. "It's nice to meet you." "Likewise," Kashi said, returning her smile and handshake as she stepped inside. Ariel took Kashi's coat and placed it inside the foyer closet. Ariel's long black hair extended past her shoulders and bounced a little as she led the way to the family room. She had deep black wide set

Imari Rogan

eyes and a beautiful brown complexion. Her make-up was perfect and she looked elegant and relaxed in a pair of jeans and sweater. Kashi noticed Ariel's high heeled designer suede boots and made a mental note that they should be shopping buddies in the future.

Reuben was sitting in front of the fireplace watching a movie on the flat screen when they entered the room. He stood up to greet her with a kiss on the cheek. "I see you met my sister Ariel." "Yes, she's very pretty." "Thank-you" beamed Ariel. "Well, if you'll excuse me, I'll let you two alone, I'm going upstairs to check on mom." When Ariel was gone, Reuben turned his attention back to Kashi and pulled her into his arms. He gazed into her eyes for a blissful moment, while taking in the beautiful scent of her signature lotion. Oh how he loved that lotion! Reuben held Kashi tightly and he didn't want to let her go. "Mmmm" he moaned, as he held her. She felt so good. Kashi rested her head on his shoulder and closed her eyes. He kissed her on the top of her forehead and she looked up at him. Their eyes locked again and they began to kiss. The chemistry between them was undeniable fire. He slid his tongue on the inside of her mouth and delicately teased her. Kashi returned his kiss with the same gentle passion. His hands moved down the length of her back, where he gently massaged away the tension of the day. He broke the kiss momentarily only to move to her neck, where he began to lightly place butterfly kisses. She tilted her head backwards to allow him to kiss her in the center of her neck. His kisses lingered in that spot for a moment before moving to the top of her chest. She tilted her head backwards toward the ceiling, as she felt herself slipping…..slipping into a place where she knew it was too soon to travel. "Oh Reuben," she managed to moan breathlessly. "Please....." He knew exactly what she was feeling and slowly broke their embrace. He understood and honored her wishes. Not now. Not here.

"I'm sorry," Reuben said, while taking Kashi's hand and leading her to take a seat next to him on the couch. "Don't be." she whispered. She didn't want him to feel guilty for what they had just experienced but she was afraid. Afraid that she was falling in love too soon with Reuben Griffin. Their hands locked as they sat close to each other. The conversation was limited. They didn't need any conversation, only each other's company. Ariel returned to the family room a moment later. Reuben and Kashi were deeply engrossed in the movie. They didn't hear her when she came in. She was grateful that Ariel hadn't come a moment sooner or she would've caught them in the act. "Hi guys," Ariel said, as she plopped down across from them on the love seat.

Imari Rogan

They looked startled when they saw her. "Good movie huh?" she asked. "Yes, it's interesting." Kashi answered, her eyes returning to the screen. Ariel noticed that their hands were locked together and decided to leave them alone. She stood to leave but Kashi stopped her. "Where are you going? Don't go." Ariel looked at Reuben. "Sit down big sis, you're not interrupting anything," he chuckled. Ariel looked relieved, took a seat and made conversation with Kashi. They talked about everything from hair, to make-up, to clothes, to treasured beauty secrets and rituals. Ariel shared a few beauty secrets about black women, while Kashi shared a few about Indian women. They seemed to have so much in common with each other. Reuben silently excused himself to go upstairs and check on their mother, while the two women got more acquainted.

Kashi learned that Ariel was 27 years old and had been married for 5 years with a 1 year old daughter. Kashi thought how lucky her husband must be to have a beautiful wife like Ariel. She seemed so pulled together. She wondered what it would be like to have Ariel for a sister in law. She chided herself. Stop it! What was she thinking? Reuben had never given her any indication that he ever wanted to marry. They chatted for a while longer before Ariel excused herself for bed. "Kashi, I really enjoyed our conversation. You're an awesome lady and I'm so glad my brother met someone like you," she said, looking in Reuben's direction, as he came back into the room. Reuben could sense that Ariel approved of Kashi, which was very unusual for his sister. She had been very picky about his past relationships. He didn't have many but Ariel had not been fond of his past girlfriends. They had all seemed like slutty little gold diggers to her, but not this time. Kashi was different and Ariel hoped they would stay together for a very long time. Kashi arose from the couch and gave Ariel a big hug. "Thanks, I enjoyed meeting you." Ariel looked over Kashi's shoulder and gave Rueben a thumbs up of approval before leaving the room. "She likes you. That's a good sign because my sister doesn't take too well to a lot of people." Kashi felt honored and uncomfortable at the same time. "Well." she sighed, "I don't want to wear out my welcome, so I'd better get going. Tell your mom I said hello" Kashi said, as she prepared to leave. "Why don't you tell her?" he asked. Before Kashi could protest, he was already pulling her hand and leading her up the spiral staircase to his mom's master bedroom. "Reuben, no!" she protested, trying to yank her hand out of his but it was too late.

They entered the bedroom as Mrs. Griffin was just starting to doze off. "Hey mom, Kashi just wanted to say goodnight, she's been visiting." Mrs. Griffin yawned and propped herself up on the king size pillows, while stifling yet another yawn. "Hello sweetheart, it's good to see you again," she said smiling. Kashi reached for her hand and took it in hers. "It's good to see you too, Mrs. Griffin, how are you feeling?" "In a lot of pain still but this too shall pass." They made small talk for a few moments before bidding each other goodnight.

Reuben walked Kashi downstairs to the front door. He pulled their coats of out of the hall foyer and walked her to her car. It was at that moment that they noticed a black SUV with black tinted windows slowly driving by. The driver was unrecognizable, due to the tinted windows but the way the car slowly cruised, it seemed as though someone was staring at them.

"Who's that?" she asked. Reuben didn't answer. He just stared at the car as it continued moving past them. "Reuben what's wrong?'" "I don't know but why is that car driving by so slowly? I don't recognize who that could be."

His mind raced back to the scratch on his car door and the prank phone call that had occurred earlier that day. He decided not to share that information with Kashi. He didn't want to upset her. He shrugged it off. "It's nothing, you'd better get home," he said, as he pulled her into his arms. He watched the car drive slowly out of the subdivision. He returned his attention to Kashi and kissed her goodnight. She hungrily returned his kiss. "Call me later," he said breathlessly. "I will," Kashi promised. "Hey what happened to your front tire?" he asked, after she had gotten in the car. "I don't know someone slashed it at the mall earlier today." She didn't sound as if she was upset. Not wanting to worry himself any further, Reuben pushed the thought from his mind. "Please make sure you get it replaced as soon as possible and don't drive on that donut too long." He tried to keep his voice calm and his face from showing any emotion but Reuben was somewhat spooked. First the scratch, than the phone call and now this. What was going on? Reuben waved goodbye as Kashi pulled out of the driveway. The black SUV was long gone. He began to think that all of these coincidences were no coincidence at all.

11

The next two months or so were somewhat uneventful. Kashi put most of her energy and time into her studies and Reuben did the same. College was proving to be a little bit tougher the more Kashi advanced into medical study. Reuben was completing his last semester of law school and would be graduating in the spring, which meant he'd no longer run into Kashi on campus. The thought of that brought him disappointment but he saw Kashi often enough and had no plans of stopping. His mom's health had been restored and she was back on her feet. Reuben was thankful that she hadn't suffered permanent brain damage. There was only a slight contusion the doctor said could have been much worse, if her head was hit in a different area.

Reuben's father was still staying at a hotel and was contemplating purchasing an apartment. He knew his family was still quite angry with him, but his mom was actually considering taking him back. They had talked on the phone a few times and he had apologized numerous times, confessed his love and promised her that nothing like this would ever happen again. Reuben was livid when his mother told him that she loved his father and may reconcile. Rueben and Ariel had sat down and discussed at length with her why they thought it wasn't such a good idea but their mother's mind was made up. She said that marriage was based on for better or for worse and that everything would eventually work itself out. She seemed confident with her decision, so her children left her alone in regards to it. However, Reuben refused to let his guard down. He would never trust his father again, when it came to his mom. He was determined to keep a watchful eye on their relationship and step in again if any problems arose. He didn't trust his father but he did trust Kashi. The time they had spent together over the last couple of months had proved to be noteworthy to say the least. He was serious about Kashi and definitely wanted her to continue to be a part of his life. Both of their schedules had been super busy over the last couple of weeks. Between classes and midterms, they hadn't seen much of each other except for the occasional lunch date in between classes.

It was one of those days during lunch they were sitting together, talking, eating, and laughing when Reuben suddenly turned serious. He reached across the table and took her hand in his. He had thought about this question long and hard and wasn't sure how she would respond. The last thing he wanted to do was scare her away.

"Kashi, I've been thinking about something." She saw the seriousness in his eyes that made her heart skip a beat. "What is it?" she

Imari Rogan

anxiously asked. "Well", he continued. "I have so much going on in my life right now with school and my family situation, among other things and I'm just tired and drained. I really think I need a break." "A break?" she asked. Oh no she thought. Was he asking for a break from her? A break from their relationship? What did she do wrong? "Yes, a break" he said, matter of factly. Kashi tried to hide her disappointment. She felt a lump began to form in her throat. Don't cry she screamed at herself. Before the tears could form in her eyes, Reuben took her hand in his. He saw that she didn't understand what he was trying to convey. "I need to get away and relax and I'd like for you to join me." It took a moment for his words to sink in. "What?" was all Kashi could manage to say. She was in total shock. He wasn't breaking up with her after all! He sounded as if he was ready to take their relationship to the next level. Kashi sat in disbelief as Reuben explained himself.

"My mom and dad own a cabin up north they purchased a few years ago. It's in a very secluded wooded area located on private property. There is a small creek behind the cabin and the area itself is simply beautiful. My mom and dad hardly ever go up there because they fight so much. The cabin has three bedrooms including a private master bedroom, three bathrooms, a fireplace, a huge country kitchen and a family room and den. I just want to get away for a weekend but I want to spend it with you. We'll both have our own separate bedrooms and I promise you that I'll be the perfect gentlemen and not force myself on you in anyway. Just think about it and let me know."

Oh my God, Kashi thought to herself. Did he just ask her to spend an entire weekend with him? She felt her cheeks flush. Spending an entire weekend with Reuben would be a dream come true but how would she manage to get away for a whole weekend? She thought about her best friend Monisha, who had her own apartment and Kashi was sure she would cover for her. She would just lie and tell her parents that she was spending the weekend with Monisha. "What weekend would you like to go?" she asked. "Next weekend if that's okay with you?" Kashi was almost breathless when she answered him. "Next weekend is fine. I'll have Monisha cover for me." "Thank you Kashi" Reuben said, holding her hand a little bit tighter. "You won't be disappointed. We're going to have a great time." And with that, he arose from his seat and kissed her on the forehead. "I'll call you later tonight." "Okay," she said. As she watched him walk out of the cafeteria, she was so nervous that she couldn't finish her meal. She threw her remaining food in the garbage and returned to class. Next weekend was only a week and a few

Imari Rogan

days away. She could hardly wait. The rest of the day went by in a haze. Kashi was floating on cloud nine until she arrived home.

As Kashi walked into the kitchen, she noticed there were two messages, written in crayon and laying next to the answering machine. Which twin was responsible? She could barely read the message. "Jessica?" she called, "come here." Jessica bounded into the room. "What?" "Did you take this message that I can't read because it's in crayon and your writing is awful." "Yeah I took it." she said, looking defensive. "I'm sorry sweetheart, what does it say?" Jessica looked at the message and translated. "It says that Logan called and he says call him back." "Thanks, Jessica" as she skipped out of the kitchen leaving Kashi looking confused.

What did he want? She had been so wrapped up in Reuben and their relationship that she had forgotten all about Logan. She had forgotten they were even still in a "relationship" too. She was supposed to be working on her feelings towards him. Kashi let out a deep sigh and dialed Logan's office number. "Dr. Roy please" she asked, when his receptionist answered the phone. "I'm sorry he's left for the day." "Thank-you." Kashi hung up and dialed his home number. "Hello?" he answered. "Hi Logan it's Kashi, how are you?" "It's been a while since I heard your voice, how are you?" "I asked you first" she said sarcastically and than she caught herself. "I'm sorry, what I meant to say is that I am just fine, how about you?" she said more cheerily. She couldn't let him think that she still despised him. "I'm okay but I would be better if I could see you." "Really?" she asked. "Yes really." She surprised herself by suggesting that they go to the movies and dinner Friday night. Logan was speechless. The phone was silent for what seemed like an eternity before she spoke again.

"Logan are you still there?' "Yes, I'm here but I just can't believe that you suggested that we go out." "Why not?' she played along, "After all we are still engaged are we not?" Kashi could hear the excitement in his voice. "Yes we are," he finally answered. "Than it's all settled, I'll see you Friday night." Logan could hardly believe his ears. "What time?' he asked cautiously. "I don't know, I guess around 7:00." "Sounds good, see you then, and Kashi?" "Yes Logan?" "I love you." Without responding, she hung up. Why did she just make a date with Logan? She had no desire to be in his company but she *had* to play along, so that he wouldn't get suspicious.

Kashi then dialed Reuben. She refused to keep secrets between them and she wanted to let him know she had made a date with Logan. She started to cry as she told him about their plans. "Reuben I just want out of this dilemma but my family will never speak to me again if I do" "Kashi, I understand your pain but just keep in mind that sooner or later, Logan is going to get tired of waiting. That's what we're hoping for, so don't get discouraged. Go out with him and try to make the best of it. It's a good look for everyone involved and no one is the wiser." "Thanks so much for understanding Reuben." "You are most welcome but most of all thanks for sharing."

12

Logan could hardly believe his luck. A date with Kashi. A date that *she* had suggested. What was going on? This was unlike her to make the first move. He was suspicious. Why the sudden change? He wondered if her feelings towards him were changing for the better. He wondered if she was actively working through her emotions, when all of a sudden out of the blue, she suggested they go out. Maybe he shouldn't be complaining and just be grateful for the fact that they were going to be together. Although he was still suspicious, Logan decided that he would be a little more reserved on their date and allow Kashi to control their conversation. In doing so, it may prove to her that he really wasn't as intimidating and pushy as she thought. Logan was going to do whatever it took to win her heart. He would give her as much time as she needed.

At 7:00, he arrived at Kashi's home. Logan checked his hair in the rearview mirror, brushed away invisible lint from his jacket collar and got out of the car. He walked slowly up the walkway and rang the bell once. No answer. He rang it a second time but still no answer. He waited patiently. He rang the bell a third time and Kashi finally answered the door. He wondered what took her so long to answer. The sight of Kashi took Logan's breath away. He wanted to take her

Imari Rogan

in his arms but resisted the impulse to do so. Besides, she was talking on her cell phone. He wondered who she was speaking to and was about to ask until he remembered that could be seen as controlling. Kashi ended the conversation telling the person on the other end that she had to go. "Who was that on the phone?" Oops! The question was out of his mouth before he could think. STUPID!! Kashi opened her mouth to answer him but he stopped her. "Please, don't answer that, it's none of my business." Kashi was taken aback. "Don't worry about it, it was just a friend." He wished that she hadn't answered him because now he wanted to know who that friend was. His jealousy got the better of him. "Who?" he asked angrily. He saw the fear in her eyes. "Logan, calm down, just a friend." He decided to let it go before he said or did something that he would later regret. "Let's not spoil the evening before it gets started." she suggested. "Okay" he quickly agreed. Logan didn't understand what was wrong with him! He had been looking forward to a nice evening and now he was ruining it. Just calm down he told himself.

They arrived at the theater and Kashi went inside to find their seats. Logan went to stand in line at the concession stand. While Logan was waiting, he had the feeling he was being watched. He quickly looked over his shoulder and noticed a young black man staring at him, who looked neither intimidating nor pleasant. They made eye contact and the man continued to stare. Logan thought that the man's behavior was a little peculiar. He was standing in the line with another man and looked as if he had no place to go. He also didn't seem interested in anything else going on around him. Logan paid for the refreshments and made his way into the theater. When he looked back, the two men were gone. As he took his seat, he thought about the man that was staring at him. He looked a little familiar. All of a sudden he remembered who he was. He turned towards Kashi. "Kashi, I think I just saw your friend Reuben in the lobby a few minutes ago." He watched her squirm in her seat and waited for her response. "Who are you talking about? she asked. "You know who...your friend Reuben." Kashi felt a little dizzy like she was going to faint. Logan had mentioned his name again. That was the second time. Kashi was afraid. Why would Reuben follow them to the movie theater? She assumed Logan must have been lying just to see if he could get a rise out of her. "I don't know what you're talking about" she said, turning away from him. "Yes you do! he yelled, as he yanked her by the arm.

The silent previews were still flashing on the screen, as people began to turn around and look in their direction. "Let me go! she demanded "or I'll leave and catch a cab home!" He loosened his grip with venom in his eyes. The lights went out and the movie started. She was dealing with a lunatic. She made a mental note to use this treatment against him in prolonging the engagement. When the movie ended, they walked to the car in silence. Once inside, Logan leaned over and kissed Kashi on the lips. She almost puked. "What are you doing?" she asked in bewilderment. "What do you think I'm doing? I'm kissing my future wife! Where to now?" he asked. "Logan if you don't mind, I'd just rather you take me home." "Home? Why home? You told me earlier that you wanted to go to dinner afterwards" "I know Logan but I changed my mind" "You little whore!" he shouted. You change your mind about *everything* don't you? Dinner? The wedding and my entire life! Who the hell do you think you are?"

Kashi responded evenly and steady, so as not to arouse any further anger "Logan, I don't appreciate you calling me names. I don't know what your problem is but you had better solve it in a hurry because I refuse to be treated this way." He was so furious that he slapped her face with an open hand. Kashi didn't know what had happened, as she found her head flying into the passenger window. Her hand flew to her cheek and her head began to spin. The tears started to stream, as she choked on her sobs. She struggled to breathe. She felt something dripping from her nose not knowing if it was mucus or blood. She wiped her nose with the back of her hand. It was blood. Hot boiling anger rose up inside of her like a pressure cooker. She lunged towards Logan and began beating him in the face with her fists. He tried to grab her wrists but she was too fast for him. She punched him relentlessly, several times in his nose and mouth. Kashi managed to hit Logan several more times before he was finally able to grab both of her arms. Logan held Kashi away from him at a distance. She saw that his nose was bleeding. He gave her a sinister smile, as if he enjoyed what was happening.

She was about to spit in his face when she heard a knock on the car window. It was the security guard. He peered into the window with his flashlight. Kashi quickly rolled the window down. "Is everything okay ma'am? Do I need to call the police?" "No" Kashi answered, while grabbing her belongings. She opened the door and quickly got out. "But will you please call an Uber for me?" "Yes ma'am" he answered, while peering at Logan and escorting her back towards the theater. People stared at her as she took a seat in the lobby. Kashi assumed that she looked horrible. The security guard was calling for an Uber from his cell phone. Kashi reached into her purse for some tissues. She wiped her nose, which was still bleeding and dabbed at her eyes. She was

Imari Rogan

shaking like a leaf. When the Uber arrived, she stood to her feet and thanked the security guard. As they drove away, she looked in the direction of where her and Logan had been parked. His car was gone. She couldn't wait to get home to tell her parents what Logan had done. She wanted them to know just how crazy he was!

13

"He did what!" Reuben yelled into the phone. Kashi was explaining to him what happened between her and Logan just a few hours earlier. She explained that Logan thought he saw Reuben standing in line at the concession stand and how he began to freak out after that. She explained how Logan had slapped her in the car and how they began to fight. "So help me God, I'll kill that mother fucker if he ever puts his hands on you again!!"

Reuben hadn't felt this much anger, since his father had hit his mom. It took a few moments for him to calm down and for Kashi to convince him not to go after Logan. Reuben explained to Kashi how he had decided to go to the movies that night with his best friend, since he didn't have any other plans. While they were standing in line waiting for refreshments, he had noticed this Indian guy looking at him over his shoulder. Reuben had no idea who he was, since he had never met Logan face to face. He had only seen him from a distance when Logan had picked Kashi up from school. Reuben had thought at the time that Logan was crazy because he kept staring at him. "Who is that?" his friend had asked. Reuben had simply shrugged. He had no idea at the time, which was a good thing because he probably would have had the urge to go into the theater and speak to Kashi. "I'm going to tell my parents what happened" Kashi said. "That's a good idea. Maybe once they know how crazy he is, they'll let you off the hook." "I'll speak with them in the morning after they have had a good night's rest." "Keep me posted," Reuben replied.

"Okay." Kashi hung up the phone and stared at the ceiling above her bed. She was tired and sleepy but knew that she wouldn't be able to sleep. Not for a while anyway. She was too upset. She got up and examined her face in the mirror. The left side of it was slightly swollen but other than that everything else looked normal. She hated Logan. How could what seemed to be the perfect guy turn into a basket case? She didn't understand. Logan had everything to lose. If she pressed charges, it would ruin his reputation and his private practice could suffer because of it. She considered this unsettling truth and than decided against it. If only she could escape from this soon to be arranged marriage, all of her troubles would be over. Kashi hoped that after tonight Logan would realize she was one who would fight back. He got a glimpse of her anger and fury and she hoped that maybe now he would consider breaking up with her. How she prayed that he would.

The next morning after breakfast, Kashi sat down with her parents in the family room. She began to explain from the first detail to the last what had happened the night before. She told them that Logan had gotten jealous of some guy he accused her of knowing and that she didn't know what he was talking about. She didn't dare tell them the truth, but she told them how he had slapped her face causing her nose to bleed and how she fought back and caught a cab home. Her parents were silent, as they took everything in that she had just said. They looked to be in shock. Her father rose to his feet and came towards Kashi to examine her face. The swelling had gone down somewhat but it was apparent that her face was still swollen. Kashi watched her father's jaw tighten in anger but he was silent. Her mother began to cry. Kashi was so sure they were going to tell her it was okay NOT to marry him but her father surprised her when he said that it had to be a logical explanation why Logan reacted that way. She couldn't believe her ears. "Dad, I just told you that he SLAPPED me. How logical is that?" "Well, you must have done or said something to him to provoke it." "So that's an excuse?!" she yelled, while jumping to her feet.

Kashi refused to believe this was happening. Her father was actually taking Logan's side. He saw the anger in Kashi's eyes and quickly tried to smooth the situation over.

"No Kashi, that is not what I meant but sometimes people lose their temper over silly little

Imari Rogan

arguments." "Dad, it wasn't a silly little argument. I simply told Logan that I wasn't hungry and to take me home and that's when he slapped me. Do you honestly think that I want to be married to someone like that?!" Her mother finally spoke up. "Kashi, please calm down. It may not be as bad as you think. Just give him another chance because he's probably under a lot of pressure from work and the stress of your postponing the wedding that he just snapped. I am sure it won't happen again." "Your mother's right... give him another chance."

Kashi looked from one to the other. This was worse than she thought. They were both willing for her to marry someone who's abusive just to satisfy a stupid tradition. She couldn't take it anymore. She ran out the room and down the hall to her bedroom, slamming and locking the door behind her. She threw herself on the bed and cried for hours. Her life was falling apart. She couldn't wait until next weekend to be with Reuben. He was the only sane person in her life right now.

****

Logan Knew that he had screwed up ...royally screwed up. Things were not supposed to turn out this way. They were supposed to go to the movies *and* dinner but Kashi hadn't been in the mood. Something had gone terribly wrong. He had lost his temper. Ordinarily, he had always been very even tempered, but last night, he had just lost it. He had surprised even himself. At the time, he didn't even recognize who he had become. It was as if he had watched the whole ordeal unfold and was an innocent bystander, who just looked on. Logan thought about how he could make up with Kashi. What could he say? What could he do? How would he convince her that he wasn't crazy? He wasn't even so sure himself anymore. Kashi. His sweet Kashi. The girl of his dreams. The woman who occupied most all of his thoughts. He wanted her. He had to have her as his wife. He was deep in thought when his phone rang. "Hello?" he answered.

"Hi Logan, its Mr. Pattel and I'd like a word with you." Logan began to get nervous. He knew that he wanted to speak with him about last night. Kashi had told him. He could hear it in her father's voice. "Yes, Mr. Pattel?" He tried to sound upbeat. "I am going to give you the benefit of the doubt THIS time but if you ever put your hands on my daughter again, it will be you and me and I will see to it that you lose everything that you stand for. Is that clear?"

"Yes it is but please let me explain." "I'm listening" said Kashi's father, obviously on the defensive.

"Kashi and I had a minor disagreement about where to go and eat dinner. She changed her mind and insisted I take her home and when I tried to convince her I wasn't ready to end the date, she became enraged and started punching me in the face. She was like a madwoman. In the process of trying to stop her, I accidentally slapped her. It was a total accident and I apologize."

He could tell that Mr. Pattel had believed his lie. "Logan" he hesitated. "I'm sorry. I guess that I just misunderstood all of this. My apologies to you. I'm sure you and Kashi will work things out over time. I'm sorry to have bothered you. Have a good day." The phone went silent. Logan hung up. He let out a sigh of relief. How gullible her father had been. He had fallen for his lie hook, line and sinker. He let out a small laugh. He was sorry that he lied but he would do whatever he had to do, to keep Kashi in his life. The last thing he wanted was to make himself an enemy to her parents. The wedding would be called off for sure if that happened. He patted himself on the back and smiled. Kashi would be his or else. He had a plan......

14

When the following weekend arrived, Kashi's bags were packed and she was prepared to leave that evening. She had lied to her parents telling them that she would be at Monisha's for the weekend. She told them she needed a change in atmosphere. Both of her parents were understanding and told her to enjoy herself.

Kashi drove to Monisha's apartment Friday night and rang the bell. Monisha greeted her at the door, with a smile and a much needed hug. They had been best friends since grade school. They knew everything about each other and shared the most intimate details of their lives, so it was no surprise when Kashi told Monisha about falling for a black guy named Reuben. Even though it was considered taboo to date someone outside of their race, Monisha was on Kashi's side when it came to Reuben. She personally didn't care about color just as long as the person was happy. Monisha knew that Logan was a jerk from the beginning. She didn't care if he was Indian or not, something just never set well with her about Logan.

As they settled into the living room, Kashi sat on the floor, took off her shoes and tucked her feet underneath her. She looked elegant and comfortable in her jeans and sweatshirt. Her long

Imari Rogan

black hair was swept up into a ponytail. She was casually comfortable and ready for the long drive to the country with Reuben. "Monisha, I just wanted to let you know that I really appreciate you covering for me this weekend, I don't know what I would do without you." "You are so welcome, that's what bff's are for." Just than the doorbell rang. Monisha got up to answer it. From where Kashi sat she could see Reuben standing in the doorway.

Monisha introduced herself and stepped aside to let him pass. Kashi stood up and greeted him with a kiss on the cheek. "I see that you guys already introduced yourselves." "Yes, and it's so nice to meet you Ms. Monisha. Thanks so much for this huge favor, we really appreciate it."

Reuben was humbled. "It's no problem at all." Monisha replied. "Ready to go?" he asked Kashi. "Yes." she said, slipping on her gym shoes and grabbing her duffle bag from the corner. "The rest of my bags are in my car." "Have fun." Monisha said. as she closed the door behind them.

Once outside, Reuben retrieved the rest of Kashi's bags from the trunk of her car and placed them inside the Range Rover. Once seated inside, Kashi breathed a huge sigh of relief. She was very grateful to be getting away. Away from all of the craziness that had gone on in their lives. Reuben's abusive father and Kashi's abusive fiancé, but for now, all that mattered was Reuben. This was going to be the perfect weekend and she refused to let thoughts of Logan spoil it for her. They were barely out of the apartment complex when Kashi received a text message.

Monisha: He's Cute

Kashi: Thanks!

Monisha: Have fun and don't do anything that I wouldn't do

Kashi: That all depends! LOL!!!

Monisha: I know! I'll let you get back to the start of a beautiful weekend. Text me when you can, if you can! LOL LOL LOL!!

Kashi: K!

The two hour drive to the northern part of the state or "up north" as it was called, was refreshing. Kashi was in seventh heaven! She and Reuben talked like old friends about everything from childhood memories to current events. They laughed and talked almost the entire time until Kashi felt herself nodding. Sleep engulfed her until she was gently nudged and awakened by Reuben, after they had arrived. When she opened her eyes, it was dark but the view of the cabin site was breathtaking and illuminated by the moonlight. It was even more beautiful than she had imagined. The cabin was surrounded by trees and a small pond was located just behind the cabin, off of a secluded road. Kashi was so glad that she had agreed to come. Reuben retrieved their bags from the car and led Kashi up the walkway. He paused for a moment to unlock the door and led her inside to the most romantic and elegant setting she had ever seen.

The living room was huge with a large fireplace on the far left wall with a white bearskin rug in front of it. The furniture was a cream colored leather sectional with three matching ottomans. There were two floor lamps on either side of the couch and several tall artificial trees lined the corners of the room. Just from where she was standing, Kashi could only imagine what the rest of the cabin would look like. It was obvious that his parents had excellent taste. "This is beautiful" she whispered, as she set her purse down. "Would you like me to show you around, since this is going to be your home away from home for the weekend?" "Sure" Kashi beamed. Reuben closed the front door behind them and then took her by the hand through the rest of the house. The living room opened into a huge dining room followed by an enormous kitchen with an island and a double sided fireplace, which the dining room and kitchen shared. There were vault ceilings throughout and the floor plan was open. Reuben then showed Kashi the master bedroom that was massive with wall to wall carpeting, a fireplace and king-size sleigh bed, which looked very inviting. The private bath had a jacuzzi tub, ceramic floors, double vanity and walk-in shower. How Kashi longed to get into that bed *right now*! This felt more like a home than a cabin. Reuben led Kashi to the other side of the cabin and showed her the guest room. Although somewhat smaller, it was just as elegant as the master bedroom. "This is where you'll be sleeping." he said. Kashi hoped that he couldn't see the disappointment in her eyes but the choice was hers. "Hungry?" he finally asked. "Yes! starving!" she admitted "Okay, have a seat in the living room and I'll go into the kitchen, unload our groceries and fix us a bite to eat." "I can't let you do all of the work yourself, so I'll help" she offered. Reuben made his way around the kitchen like a seasoned chef. They chatted while they prepared dinner. Reuben made the spaghetti and Kashi prepared the salad and garlic bread. They sat down across from each other at the table and hungrily dove into their food. "This is delicious," exclaimed Kashi. "You're a great cook." "Thank-you," he said smiling. When they finished their dinner, they returned to the living room with two bottles of iced tea and two slices of strawberry cheesecake. Reuben lit the fireplace and they sat down on the bear skin rug to enjoy their tea and dessert.

Kashi's cell phone rang. She got up and retrieved it from her purse. The number was unavailable.

She answered. "Hello?" CLICK. "That's strange," she told Reuben. "Someone just hung up on me." "You know that's been happening to me too a lot lately. I'll answer my cell and either I hear someone breathing real hard or they just hang up."

"Well let's not worry about it" she said. "I'm sure it's nothing."

She returned to her seat next to Reuben in front of the fireplace. She watched the flickering flames and soaked up the warmth that it offered. Rueben looked at Kashi in the glow of the flames. She was beautiful and radiant. He wanted her right then and there but dared not because he didn't want to lose her respect. That's what love was all about. Love...It was amazing. He knew that he loved Kashi with all of his heart. He had known since the night she had visited his mom. He hadn't been looking for love, but love had found him. He smiled within and stared into the fireplace. Kashi snuggled up against him and they sat quietly for a few moments. Each lost in their own thoughts.

"Having fun yet?" Reuben asked "As a matter of a fact I am. I've never really been on a camping trip before, so to speak. Usually when you think of camping you think of living outdoors in a tent and fishing for food or getting chased by a grizzly bear," she laughed, "but this is so much better."

"Yeah I agree," Reuben said "and I could not have asked for a better camping buddy." They both shared a laugh. They finished their cheesecake and iced tea. Reuben suggested they play a few board games that he had brought along. They went into the kitchen and sat down at the table.

The first game they played was Parcheesi and then Backgammon. That turned into Scrabble and finally Othello. During the last round of Othello, Kashi began to yawn. She was so sleepy. Reuben glanced at his watch. It was 1:00 in the morning. "Sorry Kashi but maybe we'd better get to bed, you're sleepy." "What about you?" she asked, while stifling another yawn. "Yeah, I'm tired too but not as tired as you." She nodded her head in agreement. They cleared the kitchen table together and loaded the dishwasher. "Well, I guess I will see you in the morning," Kashi said, as she turned to walk away. She could feel his eyes penetrating her backside as she walked. "Kashi wait..." Reuben whispered. He moved towards her as she turned around to face him. "May I kiss you goodnight?" he asked. "What a silly question," she murmured. As their eyes locked, so did their lips. Kashi melted into his embrace. He held her gently in his arms as their kisses became one. She could smell the scent of his cologne. Musky and alluring... sexy, yet sweet. His tongue moved inside of her mouth like it had a mind of its own and knew what to do. They felt themselves slipping and they each knew they had better stop before they went too far. It was Rueben who pulled away first.

"Goodnight" he whispered and he kissed her on top of her forehead. "Goodnight," she answered. This time when she turned and walked away, he didn't stop her. Kashi was glad because she knew that if he had stopped her again there would be no stopping either of them.

She went into the guest bedroom and softly closed the door behind her. She slowly undressed and climbed into the shower. She let the warm water cascade down her body, while enjoying the aroma of the fragranced body wash. The water felt therapeutic to her tired body, which ached for sleep. After she showered, she dried off, applied the fruity lotion that Reuben adored, slipped into her nightshirt and climbed under the covers. Sleep overtook her with a vengeance. The last thing she remembered hearing was the shower running in Reuben's room down the hall. Reuben was lost in his own thoughts, as he showered and dressed for bed. As he climbed under the covers, he realized that he wasn't sleepy. In fact, he was kind of wired up. As he lay in the bed in the dark, he stared at the ceiling and thought about Kashi. He wondered if she had fallen asleep yet. She was so close and yet so far. Kashi. What a beautiful name and what a beautiful woman! He was so blessed to have met her. Reuben was in love. Thoughts of Kashi seemed to relax his mind. Sleep kidnapped him before he even realized it.

15

How could he have let this happen? How could he have been so foolish as to get lost. This was going to throw him way off...way off schedule that is. He was on a time limit and time was of the essence concerning this situation. What was he going to do? He had no clue where to go or WHO to ask for directions. As far as he knew, he wasn't that far but exactly WHERE was the question. He sat on the side of the road for a moment and quickly remembered that he had brought his laptop along. " Big dummy," he said out loud. "I should have thought of that at first." He flipped it open and pushed the power button. The screen lit up like lightning. He punched in a few numbers and letters and found the information that he needed. He was brilliant. When he pulled off the side of the road, he pulled off with a purpose.

Kashi awoke to the smell of breakfast cooking. She rolled over and glanced at the nightstand clock. It was 10:30 a.m. She was still a little groggy from the long night before and wanted to go back to sleep, but she forced herself out of bed anyway. Besides, it would be rude not to join Reuben for breakfast. She washed up, brushed her teeth and got dressed. She looked in the mirror before going into the kitchen. She looked tired. "Good morning," she said, as she stifled a yawn. Reuben had his back turned and was busy cooking at the stove. He heard her voice and turned around. "Good Morning," he said smiling. "Can I do anything to help?" Kashi asked. "No, just sit down and relax and leave everything to me." She took a seat at the table and felt a twinge of guilt watching him cook. She got up and began to make herself busy by setting the dining room table. She walked back and forth between the kitchen and dining room, gathering silverware, napkins and plates. She carried the pitcher of orange juice into the dining room and set it in the middle of the table. By the time she was finished, breakfast was ready.

They sat down to pancakes, turkey bacon, scrambled eggs and mixed fruit. Everything looked scrumptious. As they began to eat, Kashi thought she saw a shadow walk by the kitchen window. "How many neighbors are there around here?" she asked. "Oh, about two or three different families but the cabins are so far apart that you hardly run into anyone. Why do you ask?" "Well... I think I just saw someone walk past the kitchen window." Reuben stood up abruptly, with a look of concern on his face. "Wait right here." He got up and walked into the kitchen, peered out of the window and looked from side to side. He inspected the other windows as well. He went to the back door at the kitchen entrance and stepped outside. He carefully looked around and didn't see anyone or anything unusual...only the bright sun on a cold day, surrounded by the woods. He looked along the perimeter of the house and didn't notice any footprints either. Reuben stepped back inside and closed the door. "I didn't see anyone" he said, sitting back down. "I'm sorry, maybe it was just my imagination," Kashi said "Maybe, but we can't just take things like that for granted. I'd rather be safe than sorry." They returned their attention to their breakfast and started making plans for the day. Kashi wanted to go hiking and Reuben wanted to go into town and get a movie rental for later that night. They decided to do both. After breakfast, they climbed into the Range Rover and drove into town. They rented a couple of movies, one scary and the other a love story. On the way back from the video store, they stopped for gas before heading back to the cabin. Once inside, they both put on their hiking boots, grabbed their backpacks and were off again to explore the woods. They hiked about a span of a half mile before stopping to take a break. They sat down on a nearby tree stump and drank a couple of bottled waters they had brought along.

"Are you tired yet?" Reuben asked. "Yes, a little," Kashi answered, somewhat out of breath.

"Well, I'll make sure that you get plenty of rest when we get back to the cabin. You can relax while I cook dinner." "No," she protested. "You cooked dinner last night, so tonight it's my turn."

"If you insist my love." My love? Did he just say my love?! Kashi felt her face flush. She tried to play off what he just said by taking another sip of water and looking away. It didn't work. He gently turned her face towards his and softly kissed her on the forehead. He pulled her into his arms and hugged her tightly. She melted in his embrace. She wanted this moment to last forever. It felt so good for him to hold her but then all of a sudden, she felt very uncomfortable….eerily uncomfortable. It felt almost as if someone was watching them. She ignored her feelings, wriggled out of his embrace and took a quick look around. Not wanting to arouse his suspicion, Kashi announced, "Last one to the cabin is a rotten egg!" She giggled as she got up and ran away. Reuben chased after her. They half ran and half walked back to the cabin. She was having so much fun just being in his company and right now they were acting like silly little teenagers. She could not have asked the universe for a better boyfriend.

They were both out of breath when they returned to the cabin. Kashi's feet were sore and hurting and so was Reuben's but the hike had been worth it. She kicked off her hiking boots in the kitchen landing and plopped down on the living room sofa. "How about a foot massage?" Reuben asked, as he entered the room. "Sure!" Kashi replied. Reuben took a seat on the floor in front of her and pulled off her socks. He began to gingerly massage her feet, which were sore and achy. Reuben's hands were working magic. Kashi closed her eyes and moaned as she lay her head back on the sofa.

"Hmmmm....don't stop," she whispered. He continued to massage the soreness out and it felt amazingly good. She didn't remember much of anything else until Reuben gently shook her awake. "I'm all done." "Oh my God, did I fall asleep?!" "Yes, you did but that's okay. I understand. You're tired." "Okay, well now it's your turn." Reuben positioned himself on the couch and Kashi got on the floor in front of him and began his foot massage. She noticed he had remarkably soft feet for a man. Not at all rough and scaly like her dad's feet. She giggled inwardly. She kneaded and massaged them until she felt his body relax. After a few minutes, he was fast asleep. She quietly got up and grabbed a throw from across the love seat. She sat down next to him and covered them both with the blanket. She lay her head on his chest and joined him in a nap.

Kashi was the first to awake. They must have slept for a few hours because when she awoke, the whole cabin was engulfed in darkness.

She sat up and gazed at Reuben. His mouth was gaped open and he was snoring loudly. Kashi laughed to herself and carefully got up, so as not to awaken him. She tiptoed into the kitchen and turned the lights on. She went into the nook to pull the blinds together that led to the deck outside. She could have sworn that she saw a figure in the distance but as Reuben had said, the neighbors were few and far between. She shrugged it off as the figure being a deer or some other wild animal. After all, they were way up north in the country. She closed the blinds and returned to the kitchen to start on dinner, which would be really simple. Frozen pizza and fresh tossed salad. She prepared the salad as the oven preheated. She could still hear Rueben snoring in the living room. She placed the pizza in the oven and took a seat at the kitchen island. She grabbed her cell phone and sent Monisha a text.

Kashi: Hey, what are you doing?

Monisha: That's not the question. What are you doing and why are you sending
me a text? Don't you have better things to do? LOL

Kashi: As a matter of a fact I do, BUT Reuben is sleeping right now and I just put a pizza in the oven, so I thought I'd check in with you…

Monisha: All is well on this end. Are you having fun yet?

Kashi: OMG! Yes! We went hiking earlier today. Had a great time. Going to eat dinner soon and watch a couple of movies.

Monisha: Sounds good!

Kashi: Yes. I'm going to wake him in a few minutes and finish the rest of our evening but I just wanted to let you know that ever since we've been here, it feels as though someone is watching us. Almost like we are not totally alone.

Monisha: I'm sure it's your imagination! Now stop texting me and go back to your weekend!

Kashi: LOL! Okay! Talk soon.

Kashi screamed, the phone flew out of her hand and across the room, as she suddenly felt two arms wrapped around her waist. It was Reuben. "Whoa!" he exclaimed. "What's wrong with you? It's me, Reuben!" Kashi was almost trembling. The figure in the dark had her spooked. She tried to laugh it off. "I'm sorry Reuben, I don't know what got into me" she said, as he went to retrieve her phone from the other side of the kitchen. He examined the screen. "Well, at least it's not broken." he said, handing the phone back to her. "Yes, I had just sent a text to Monisha and I didn't hear you behind me." She explained to him what she thought she had seen moments ago, when she pulled the blinds. Reuben pulled Kashi into his arms and looked deeply into her eyes. "Don't let what happened this morning spook you out. I'm here with you and you're safe and sound. I would never let anything happen to you."

"Okay." she whispered. The moment was interrupted by the beeping of the oven timer. She retrieved the pizza from the oven and a few moments later, they were enjoying dinner and conversation. The eerie feeling that Kashi had felt earlier had all but vanished now. After dinner, Reuben lit the fireplace and they settled on the couch once again to watch the movies. As they engrossed themselves with the characters on screen, they didn't hear as someone was trying the doorknob at the back door..............

****

Oh wow!! That was so stupid he thought to himself. Why was he trying to get in through the back door?! Had his senses totally left him? Didn't he know and realize that they were STILL INSIDE? The Range

Rover was right there in the driveway! What was he thinking? As soon as he tried to turn the knob, which by the way didn't budge, he quickly ducked down out of view, just in case one of them had heard it. He had almost been caught earlier and he didn't need to risk it again. He should have done what needed to be done, when they had gone on their hiking expedition but now he feared it was too late. His leg began to cramp from ducking down so low for so long but he had to be sure that the coast was clear. After for what seemed like hours, he slowly stood to his feet. He walked about a half mile back to his car and made a phone call.

16

The last movie was scary. A serial killer was on the loose in a remote town. There was a scene where a couple was taking a shower together and the killer came in with a knife and stabbed them both to death. Kashi screamed and jumped through most of the movie but Reuben just laughed at her. "It's not funny!" she said, jabbing him on the arm. "Yes it is, you know it's not real." He had tears in his eyes from laughing so hard.

"Well, it may not be real but it could be!" she argued. She thought again about the incident at the window but tried to push the thought from her mind. Deep down inside she didn't want to sleep alone tonight, not with everything that had transpired that day. She felt uneasy. Sensing her fear, Reuben pulled her into his arms. Without another word, he kissed her passionately on the lips. His tongue found its familiar place within the crevices of her mouth and her tongue mingled with his, as if they had a language of their own.

Soon, she found herself lying on her back within the comfort of the deep sofa cushions, as Reuben lay on top her. His lips moved to her chin and found their way to her neck. Kashi thought back to the moment at his home in the family room, where he had planted the same type of kisses in the same spots that night. The only difference tonight was there was no one there to interrupt their privacy. They were all alone and only had to answer to themselves.

He moved his head to the top of her chest and just shy of pulling up her t-shirt, he abruptly stopped. Kashi opened her eyes at the sudden interruption. He looked up at her with a look of disappointment yet certainty. "I'm sorry Kashi but I made you a promise that I intend to keep. Prior to this weekend, I told you I would be the perfect gentlemen and not coerce you into anything you may not be ready for." Without waiting for her response, he abruptly kissed her on the forehead and told her goodnight. "I'll see you in the morning," Reuben whispered and with that he simply walked to his bedroom and closed the door. Kashi was left lying in the dark that was only illuminated by the fireplace. She stared at the ceiling a few moments thinking about what he had just said. She could still smell the scent of his musky cologne that still permeated in the air. She inhaled deeply before finally getting up and walking to her room.

She showered and climbed into bed. She was restless…..absolutely restless. She wasn't pleased with how the evening had ended but she respected how Reuben was a man of his word. He didn't just take it upon himself to have sex with her the way that Logan had. At least he was taking it slow. She peered out of the bedroom window into the darkness and watched the shadows of the trees sway in the moonlight. It wasn't Reuben who had changed his mind but it was Kashi. She got out of bed walked down the hall to Reuben's room in her bare feet and nightgown. She knocked quietly on the door. It took a moment for him to answer. Maybe he was sleeping. As she started to walk away, the door opened. He stood in the middle of the doorway wearing only pajama bottoms. His bare chest was muscular and almost had a sheen to it. Her eyes quickly traveled down the length of his pajama pants and back up again. Their eyes met. Kashi moved towards him and he took her in his embrace.

"I don't want to be alone tonight." she whispered. "Then you don't have to be." He took her by the hand, led her into the bedroom and closed the door behind them. He lay on the bed and pulled her on top of him. He kissed her with unbridled passion and she returned his kisses with the same urgency. She paused for a brief moment, pulled her nightgown over her head and tossed it somewhere besides them. Reuben lay back and stared at her bare breasts. He reached up and placed his hands over them and began a tender massage. He sat up and began to kiss and suck them passionately one at a time. Kashi threw her head back and enjoyed the moment. She moaned with sweet desire. He placed her on her back and climbed on top of her, never missing a beat with where he had left off. He kissed her everywhere he could think of. Her lips, her breasts, her neck and her belly before moving down to her forbidden area. The only light in the room was the moonlight that poured in from the bay windows but he could still see the beauty of her body. She was simply exquisite. He allowed his hands to stroke the length of her body, as he gently kissed her thighs. He restrained himself from going any further, He would save that for another time. Reuben moved up to kiss Kashi's lips and when he paused, he asked her if she wanted him to stop.

"No" It was a breathless whisper. She didn't want him to stop now or ever. She sensed her insides quivering and felt the moisture building up from deep within her, that threatened to escape at any moment. Reuben removed his pajama bottoms and tossed them on the floor besides the bed. Kashi could feel his manhood against her naked thighs, as they kissed like never before. She opened her legs as he eased himself inside of her, while he softly moaned her name. She wrapped her legs around his waist, so she could take in every inch of him leaving nothing to the imagination. Unlike the night with Logan, tonight she was the aggressive one. They rocked back and forth in unison like an old romantic love song.

Slowly at first and than gradually accelerating. She let her mind drift back to her senior year in high school, where she and a few friends were in the locker room discussing orgasms and what they felt like. Kashi hadn't been ashamed to admit that she was a virgin at the time and had no idea what an orgasm was, let alone how one felt. Her friends had giggled and told her that she was truly missing out. She was also absolutely sure that she had not had one with Logan. But now as she felt her entire body slowly tremble and a feeling of the most intense pleasure overtake her, tears of joy began to stream. Kashi climaxed and her body rocked with his and continued to shake throughout. It was long and rhythmic, as she cried and wailed and moaned. She had absolutely no control of how her body was reacting and to be quite honest, she didn't care. It felt extremely pleasurable, yet frightening at the same time. She struggled to catch her breath, as her legs and hands continued to tremble. Reuben , sensing what was happening, cradled her in his arms. "It's okay Kashi" he whispered "just let it go, let go." As he watched the look of pleasure on her face, he began to feel the pressure of his own climax building. He began to lose control and Kashi wrapped her legs even tighter around his waist to meet his thrusts, as he exploded. He let out a long guttural moan with a sigh of relief.

A moment later he moved beside Kashi and pulled her into his arms. Their bodies glistened with sweat and they were breathless, as they lay quietly next to each other. Kashi's head rested on his chest. Reuben was the first to speak. "I love you Kashi." She felt a lump rise up in her throat as she tried to choke back tears. It was as if every dream she had of falling in love was coming true but not with the person that she was engaged to. For the first time Kashi was following her heart. "I love you too Reuben ." she whispered. And with that she let the tears flow. This is what REAL love felt like and it was the best feeling in the world. Reuben was nervous regarding what he was about to ask BUT he knew in his heart what he wanted. He knew that he loved Kashi with all of his heart. He knew it the moment at his parent's house, when he held her close. The one thing his father had always told him was that if a man truly loved a woman, it shouldn't take forever to make up his mind to spend the rest of his life with her. There was no need to prolong what was inevitable.

"Kashi, would you please marry me?" She lay motionless for a moment not believing what she had heard. The tears now flowed freely, as she began to cry and almost sob. Before she could answer, Reuben reached for the black velvet box that was tucked away in the nightstand drawer. He opened it to reveal the most elegant diamond engagement ring that Kashi had ever seen. She was still crying, as he placed the ring on her finger. Her hand flew up to her mouth to stifle the cries that were coming. What was she going to do? What was she going to say? When would Logan finally be out of her life for good, so that she could really start living her life? Reuben knew that this decision may not be easy for Kashi. "Please don't let me place any added pressure on you but I just thought you should know where I stand. I bought the ring a couple of months ago. I knew then that I loved you but I wanted us to take our time. I had to be sure that you felt the same way about me. It was important that our feelings were mutual. I know Logan is a problem but we will deal with that situation one day at a time. In the meantime, I'll wait for you. I'll wait as long as it takes but not without knowing that I have your heart and that you have mine"

She shook her head yes while falling into his embrace. "Yes Reuben yes, I'll marry you!" They laughed and cried and held each other tightly never wanting the moment to end. "Kashi's mind was made up. When she returned home after this weekend, she was going to tell her parents that the wedding was off. She was no longer willing to be miserable for everyone else to be happy. This life that she lived belonged to her and she had every right to live it. Her parents would disown her but it would be so worth it to be free. Enough was enough.

17

Sunday morning arrived too soon. The bright sunlight streamed through the huge bay windows slightly nudging Kashi awake. She blinked a few times to allow her eyes to adjust to the daylight. She stirred a little and realized she was still wrapped in Reuben's arms. The musky aroma of their lovemaking still lingered in the air around them. The smell was alluring, sexy and sensual. It made her want him again. She stretched her left arm out in front of her to gaze at her engagement ring. It sparked brightly in the sunlight. The diamond was huge. She could only imagine how much it must have cost him. It was obvious that he had put much time and thought into it. She sighed softly and snuggled closer to Reuben. His body heat mingled with hers, as they lay underneath the goose down comforter. She lay quietly as she listened to his snoring. She wondered what time it was.

After a few minutes, she slowly and gently eased herself from his embrace and got out of bed. He didn't budge. He was a hard sleeper. She tiptoed into the master bathroom and closed the door behind her. She stepped into the shower and lathered herself up. The shower revived her senses and gave her a newfound energy. Her body had been spent from last night. She wrapped herself in a bath towel and walked down the hallway to retrieve her clothing for the day ahead. Reuben never moved. She brushed her teeth at the bathroom sink and sat down on the side of the bed to apply the sweet smelling body lotion that Reuben adored. Just then she heard the shower running down the hall. She smiled to herself as she rummaged through her luggage to find what she would wear. She chose a pair of jeans and her favorite cashmere sweater. A Christmas present that Logan had gifted her with two years ago. She quietly giggled to herself, as she lay the clothes to the side and stepped into her bra and panties. Just the thought of her wearing something that Logan had given her and here she was with someone else. That was very funny to her.

All of a sudden there was that feeling again. She felt as if she was being watched. She whirled around only to find Reuben standing in her doorway completely naked. His body was glistening from the shower he had just taken. He hadn't even bothered to dry himself fully off. His eyes were burning with love and passion. No words were needed. They made their way into each other's embrace. Their tongues intertwined, as her hands found their way to his buttocks. She gently squeezed, as she allowed his hands to remove her panties. She reached backwards and unhooked her bra. She tore it off and tossed it to the side. She massaged his manhood as a deep

Imari Rogan

moan escaped his throat. Kashi sat down on the edge of the bed as Reuben braced himself between her legs and lifted them above his shoulders. He pushed himself inside of her and she cried out. It was a mixture of pleasure and pain but the pain was oh so good to her. They made love with unbridled passion and the climax they shared brought a satisfaction to be remembered.

****

After their lovemaking session had ended, they showered again and ate a late breakfast. By the time they returned the movie rentals to the video store, it was way past noon. They were charged a late fee but it had been so worth it. They returned to the cabin to clean up and pack their belongings for the trip back home. Kashi was super sad. She didn't want the weekend to end. She quietly swept and mopped the kitchen floors and washed and put all of the dishes away. Reuben was busy vacuuming the living room floors and washing and drying the bed linens. As Kashi was packing the last of her things in her luggage, she heard Reuben calling her from what seemed like outside. She could hear the panic in his voice. She dropped what she was doing and ran to the back door. When she stepped outside, she saw it. Someone had thrown a brick through the passenger window of the Range Rover and the brick was laying on the ground, with a typed written note, secured with a rubber band. Reuben was standing next to the broken glass scattered in the driveway, shaking his head in disbelief. "Who would do something like this?" he asked to no one in particular.

His eyes searched back and forth between the Range Rover and the surrounding property, looking for the perpetrator. Kashi's hands began to tremble, as she walked towards the brick and picked it up. She carefully unwrapped the note and read it aloud.

"I sincerely hope the two of you enjoyed your weekend rendezvous. This is just a little token of my observation and appreciation." She felt her insides turn to jelly and a wave of dizziness over take her. The note slipped out of Kashi's hands and Reuben caught her before she hit the ground. Kashi had fainted. He carried her into the cabin and lay her down on the couch. He got a cold compress from the kitchen and placed it on her forehead just as she was coming to.

"What happened?" Kashi asked, while struggling to sit up. "Just relax, you passed out." Reuben continued to wipe her forehead with the compress.

Kashi tried to get her thoughts together but she was absolutely stunned at what had just taken place. Somehow she knew in her heart that

Imari Rogan

Logan was behind everything. Reuben took a seat next to her and let out a long sigh. "I have something to tell you." "Okay, I'm listening," as Kashi looked at him expectantly. "Well" he said, taking a deep breath. "Do you remember when we first arrived Friday night and you got a hang up on your cell phone?" "Yes, I remember."

"Well, do you also remember me telling you that I had a couple of hang ups too?" "Yes, I remember that too." "Well, there's something else that I didn't tell you because I overlooked it until now. The day that I picked my mother up from the hospital, I noticed that someone had keyed the Range Rover. It looked intentional. At first I shrugged it off but then as we were on our way home, someone called from an unavailable number and when I answered they hung up." Reuben looked at Kashi waiting for her response. She leaned back on the cushions and thought about everything that she had just been told. She was now beginning to put two and two together.

She sat up and turned to face him squarely in the eye. She sighed. "Well, I guess there's something that I need to tell you too." Now it was Reuben who sat at attention. Kashi nervously rubbed her hands together, as she began to tell her side of the story. "The same day that you picked up your mother from the hospital, I went shopping with the twins at the mall. We shopped just about all afternoon and when we returned to the parking lot, someone had slashed my tire on the driver's side. I called roadside service to fix the tire and the mechanic asked me if I had any enemies because the tire had been deliberately slashed." Kashi stared at the floor when she was finished. Reuben sounded annoyed when he replied. "Kashi you should have told me!" "Yes, I agree I should have told you but you didn't tell me either what was going on with you!" she snapped. Reuben quickly grabbed her hand and kissed it.

"I'm sorry sweetheart, we won't fight about it. It's obvious that we've been spooked enough. It is what it is but someone is out to get us." he said. "I agree, and I think we both know who." Reuben nodded his head in agreement. He paused for a moment before responding. "What I would like to know is how he found us? How did he know we were here?" "I don't know," Kashi responded, "but what I do know is that this must just be his sick way of trying to scare me but it won't work. I'm already in love with you and I'm committed to you." He kissed the top of her forehead. "I love you too and I refuse to let him intimidate us. We may have to get some type of restraining order against him, but in the end we would have to prove that it's Logan and that he is actually a real threat. What if it isn't him?" "Trust me, it is." Kashi said, with anger in her eyes.

Imari Rogan

She arose from the couch with determination in her voice. "Let's get this glass cleaned up and finish getting ready to leave." Reuben grabbed the broom and dustpan from the closet and went outside to clear the debris from the driveway. Kashi found some heavy plastic in the laundry room to cover the car window until they could make it somewhere for the repair.

The drive home was cold and miserable from the makeshift window covered in plastic. They tried to make light hearted conversation but it was no use. They were both worried about what happened and they were freezing cold, despite the heat being turned all the way up. When they arrived at Monisha's apartment, Kashi was coughing and sneezing. She had body aches and felt horrible. She couldn't afford to be sick. She had classes tomorrow. Reuben transferred Kashi's luggage to the trunk of her car and asked her if she was going home. "Not this minute, I'm going to go and tell Monisha what happened and thank her for looking out for me."

"I'll go with you," Reuben replied. Once inside, Monisha's smile faded when she saw the look of disappointment on their faces. "What happened to you guys?" she asked, while offering them a seat. They all sat down and Kashi brought Monisha up to date about all of the bizarre things that had been happening to her and Reuben, including the broken car window at the cabin. Although Monisha was somewhat taken aback, she wasn't at all surprised. She looked pointedly at Kashi as she spoke. "Well to be honest Kashi, I always had a bad feeling about Logan and this proves it." "Why do you say that?" Kashi asked. "Well, just because…he always gave me the creeps. Like the time we double dated last year and Logan refused to let you out of his sight. He clung to you like a magnet and when we left to go to the ladies room, he asked you what took us so long. I never mentioned it to you at the time but Logan is very possessive of you and that's not good. I even caught him sneaking around my parking lot a few weeks ago. I just happened to be looking out the window and I recognized his car. He was slowly driving around, as if he was looking for something or someone. I started to text you but I knew you were out with Reuben and I didn't want to scare you. He was probably checking up on you then, trying to figure out where you were."

Kashi was stunned. Reuben arose from his seat with anger. He jammed his fists into the pockets of his jeans and began to pace the floor. "That bastard! he jeered. "What do you think I should do?" Kashi asked. Monisha glanced at Reuben, who was still pacing back and forth. "I don't know Kashi but if Logan is behind all of this, the two of you need to be extra careful. I have no idea what he's capable of but I don't think that he's willing to give you up without a fight. Logan is crazy."

Kashi couldn't take anymore. She buried her face in her hands and broke down crying. Monisha reached out to her and took her in her arms. "Don't cry sweetie, just be careful, I'm sure things may not be as bad as we think but just to be on the safe side, you guys should lay low for a while." Reuben sat down on the couch on the other side of Kashi. He stroked the back of her hair. "Don't worry babe, I won't let anything happen to you. If he so much lays one finger on you, I'll kill him." Reuben meant every word that he said. He wasn't about to take any of Logan's crap. He loved Kashi and would die for her if he had to. Kashi regained her composure and finally stood to leave. "I'm going home and get some rest, thanks again Monisha, I'll call you later Reuben." Monisha gave Kashi a final hug before walking her to the door. Monisha stopped in her tracks and gasped. She couldn't help but notice the ring on Kashi's finger. "Wait a minute!" Monisha squealed. "That's NOT the ring that Logan gave you!"

Kashi felt the happiness return to her weary soul. She smiled again for the first time in hours. "No, it's not," she responded. "Reuben proposed to me last night." Monisha laughed with joy as she gave Kashi another giant hug. "I'm so happy for you guys!" She hugged Reuben too. "Thanks Monisha" Reuben said smiling. "Well, please be careful and if I see Logan sneaking around here again I'll let you know." Kashi was paranoid. Once outside, she kept looking over her shoulder. Reuben walked her to her car and waited until she was settled in. She waved goodbye as she drove out of the lot. As Reuben stood waving in the background, she could have sworn she saw Logan's black Mercedes Benz lurking in the dark shadows of the parking lot.

Imari Rogan

18

Kashi lay in bed Monday morning with a fever, body aches and chills. She had been forced to miss class. She was just too sick. She slept off and on during the day and tried to nurse herself back to health with chicken soup, jello and aspirin. By noon, she felt somewhat better but not so much. She rolled over in bed and went back to sleep. Minutes later, Kashi was awakened by her cell phone. She reached for it from the nightstand and answered. "How are you feeling? I'm sitting in the cafeteria all alone." It was good hearing Reuben's voice. Kashi smiled into the phone. "I feel horrible and I had to stay home, how are you?" "Better now that I'm talking to you. Can I bring you anything?" "No, I'm fine and besides you know that you can't come to my home, my parents would have a fit" "I know but sooner or later they'll have to meet me, since you're going to be the future Mrs. Griffin," he chuckled. "Mrs. Griffin," she sighed. "I love that name already," Kashi giggled.

"I just wish that everything wasn't so complicated. My parents are so prejudiced. They are pro-Indian about everything." "I know how you feel," Reuben agreed. "Unfortunately there are those that are just set in their ways. Blacks against whites, whites against blacks, blacks against arabic, arabic against blacks, Indians against blacks. The list goes on and on. it's unfair but that's the way it is. When I first met you, I didn't care that you were Indian. The only thing that I could see was a beautiful woman, who would be my future wife." "I love you Reuben," Kashi whispered. "And I love you. We'll be okay one way or another. Your parents will eventually come around. We'll just take one day at a time. Look, I gotta get back to class but get some rest and I'll call you later."

Kashi lay back down and drifted into a deep slumber. She started to dream. She was dreaming of her wedding day with Reuben. They were standing on the beach all dressed up but in their bare feet. Kashi's white wedding gown blew softly in the wind, as she gazed into Reuben's eyes. He looked so handsome in his black tuxedo. A minister was standing in front them and reciting their vows from a small black book. They smiled at each other but the wedding was interrupted by what sounded like gunfire. Kashi awoke with a start. There was the sound again but it wasn't gunfire. Someone was banging hard on the front door. She sat straight up. Her headache had returned with a vengeance. She slipped on her robe and house slippers and slowly made her way to the door. Without looking out of the peephole first, she opened it and there stood Logan in front of her, boiling with anger. He was holding his briefcase and a large manila envelope in his hand.

He pushed his way past her and without a word, he walked into the living room and slammed the envelope onto the coffee table. He was breathing hard, as if he had just finished completing a marathon. She thought about running to her room, locking the door and calling the police but fear made her stand frozen in her tracks. She closed the door behind her and slowly walked towards Logan. She said nothing but kept her distance. He was wearing his hospital scrubs and lab coat, so she assumed he had just left his office. Logan stared at her through squinted eyes. "Are you going to invite me to have a seat? he shouted. "Of course Logan, please have a seat." Kashi tried to keep her voice calm and steady. What was he doing here? How did he know she was home? Fear gripped her even more, as he plopped down on the couch and patted the seat beside him. She remained standing where she was, just in case she had to make a run for it. "How may I help you?" she asked. He ignored her question. "Aren't you feeling well Kashi?" Sarcasm laced his voice. "No, I'm not, I think I have the flu." "Aww, that's too bad." Logan said, mockingly. "Let me examine you," he ordered, as he stood to approach her. "Logan please don't come near me." Kashi said, in a stern voice. She was super afraid but stood her ground. Her hands began to shake. She shoved them into the pockets of her robe and shifted her weight from one foot to the other. She looked nervously towards the floor. How she wished her parents or the twins or anyone would come home at this moment.

"I have something I need to discuss with you and I need your undivided attention, so come over here and sit down." Logan demanded. Kashi did as she was told but she sat across from him on the love seat. "I'm listening" she managed to say. "Kashi", he began, "First of all, I need you to know that I am not the idiot that you think I am." "What are you talking about?" as Kashi tried her best to sound dumbfounded. "You know damn well what I'm talking about but just in case you don't, let me explain everything to you," he paused, before starting again. "I know all about you and Reuben". He searched her face for a glimmer of guilt. "I never told you his name." "You didn't have to because I hired a private detective a few months ago to follow you after you broke up with me that day at the park. Do you remember?" Logan looked like the psychopath that he was, sitting across from her. Kashi felt stomach bile rising in her throat. Don't get sick now she said to herself. "Logan I told you then that our breakup had nothing to do with him." Kashi pleaded with her eyes for him to stop this nonsense. "LIAR!" he screamed. Logan was so angry that his hands were trembling. His nostrils flared and his jaw tightened, as he continued. "I hired a private detective. The best

Imari Rogan

that the state has to offer. He went not only above the call of duty but beyond it. I now know Reuben's first and last name, his date of birth, his address, his cell phone number, his license plate number and a thing or two about some of his close relatives." Kashi knew Logan was telling the truth because that would explain the hang ups, the slashed tire, the broken window and everything else. "Logan, why are you doing this?" Kashi was now in tears. She was absolutely terrified of what he might do next. "You have the nerve to ask me why?" he barked. "I'll tell you why." Logan paused for a moment before reaching for the envelope. He threw it at her. "OPEN IT!" he demanded. With trembling hands, Kashi picked up the envelope from the floor where it had landed. She could only imagine what was inside. She pulled the contents out and held them for a moment before looking at them. She stared long and hard at Logan before letting her eyes drift to the papers.

What she saw next literally snatched her breath away. She began to gasp for air. She felt as if she was choking and suffocating all at the same time. He watched her sink to the floor on her knees. "Breathe bitch!" he shouted. Kashi was having a full blown panic attack. She doubled over and in an attempt to catch her breath, she dropped the contents on the floor. "Oh God" she sobbed. She gripped her chest and her breath came out in rapid short bursts. For a moment, Logan thought she might be having a heart attack but he didn't move. "Kashi" he said, in an evenly sinister and calm voice. "Get a hold of yourself and take deep breaths s-l-o-w-l-y" Kashi followed his instructions because she was too afraid not to. She thought she was dying. "Keep breathing in and out slowly." After a few minutes, her breathing eventually returned to normal but she was far from okay. She managed to drag herself from the floor and return to her seat. She sat very still with a blank look on her face. "Pick up the pictures and look at them, NOW!" he screamed. She couldn't believe this was happening. This had to be a nightmare… one that she couldn't wake from. She picked the pictures up from the floor and forced herself to view them. The photos had been developed on 8 x 10 glossy paper, live and in color. The first photo was of her and Reuben saying goodbye to each other from their first date at the coffee shop. The next few photos were of her and Reuben, taken from various angles at the hotel on Christmas night. The next one was of them kissing in the parking lot that same night. The next photo had been taken outside of Reuben's house the night Kashi had come to visit his mother. They were standing close to each other talking. The most devastating of all came next. As Kashi looked at the last of the photos, she almost went into hysterics.

Imari Rogan

She began to cry again. "OH NO OH NO" she wailed. There were six pictures of her and Reuben at the cabin. They must have been taken from the bedroom window. Kashi and Reuben were making passionate love in different positions. She threw the pictures on the floor, buried her face in her hands and sobbed uncontrollably. Logan showed no remorse. He just watched her cry. When she finally looked at him, he had a sly wicked smirk on his face. "What do you want from me Logan, why are you doing this? "If I can't have you than no one else will. You were promised to me and I won't be denied. You're mine...period. You WILL marry me. It doesn't matter to me that you slept with some nigger because that nigger will soon be history.

He waited for her to respond. "What do you mean be history? "I simply mean that you will break it off with him and our wedding will go on as planned. If not, I'll take the photos and show them to your parents. Once they find out, they will be more than happy to disown you knowing that their daughter is nothing more than a tramp, who sleeps with niggers!" Her mouth flew open in surprise. He was crazy. Really crazy and he meant every word of his threat. "That's blackmail" Kashi said in a voice barely above a whisper. "You're blackmailing me." "Call it what you want. Break it off with that nigger and tell your parents the wedding is no longer on hold. I expect that after this, our lives will go on as normal as a regular couple. If not, I promise you that life as you know it will never be the same." Logan stood and snatched the photos from the floor and returned them to the envelope. "It was YOU who slashed my tires, keyed Reuben's car and who threw the brick through the car window at the cabin and all of the prank calls then" He neither confirmed nor denied what she said. He simply placed the envelope in his briefcase and walked towards the door. "Have a good day my future wife" Logan said, before giving Kashi a quick kiss and walking out. Kashi picked up the crystal vase from the foyer table and threw it at the door as it closed. It shattered into a million pieces.

****

Logan felt complete. He felt elated. He felt victorious. Now he knew his plan was working. He was convinced that once they were married, everything would change for the better. Kashi was his world, his life and his everything. He didn't care about Reuben's attachment to Kashi...all he cared about was his own. When Logan returned to work, the receptionist handed him several messages and a few patient files that had accumulated while he was gone. Logan stepped into his office and closed the door. He sat down at his desk and reclined in his leather chair. It felt good to be in charge again. He thought about how well his plan had worked. He prided himself in doing such a good job. The only thing that wasn't planned was the course of action that he'd taken upon himself, each time his private investigator reported back to him. It wasn't his intent at first, to take his keys and drag them down the side of Reuben's car but he couldn't help himself. "Bob," as he preferred to be called, had notified Logan of every move that Kashi and Reuben made. Bob had followed Reuben to the hospital and promptly reported every detail to Logan. What Bob wasn't aware of was that each time he told Logan about their whereabouts, Logan would go to the said location and cause property damage. If Bob had been aware of Logan's actions, he would have quit the case on the spot. Logan's behavior was unethical. But what Bob didn't know wouldn't hurt him, even when Logan had slashed Kashi's tires, with a surgical scalpel.

The ultimate revenge came when they spent this past weekend at the cabin. Bob had called Logan from the side of the highway and told them where they were. Logan had instructed him to take as many photos as possible and to bring them to him as soon as possible. For the entire weekend, Logan hadn't been able to rest. He could only imagine what his bride to be would be doing, while in the arms and company of another man. The photos were dropped off early Sunday morning and after reviewing them carefully, Logan had gotten in his car and drove the two hour ride to the cabin site. When he arrived, he saw the Range Rover in the driveway but couldn't risk being seen. He drove about a quarter mile away from the cabin and parked on the side of the road. He retrieved the brick and the pre typed written note from the back seat and walked the short distance to the cabin. He hid behind the bushes in the driveway and carefully glanced in the huge kitchen window to see any signs of life. Satisfied that no one was watching, he reached from behind the bushes, threw the brick at the Range Rover and ducked back out of sight. Logan was sure Kashi and Reuben would have heard the loud crash, with all of the glass that had broken. Luckily for him, the car alarm wasn't set. He waited a few minutes and still when no one came outside, he ran back through the wooded area, returned to his car and sped away.

As Logan reached into his briefcase and examined the pictures again, he imagined that it was himself in those pictures with Kashi instead of Reuben. The look of ecstasy on her face let him know that she was enjoying every moment of their love making. He wondered if he could ever satisfy her the way that Reuben did. He felt himself stiffen beneath his trousers and his hand moved to his manhood. Not now he told himself. His office was not the place for self gratification. He told himself that it would only be a matter of time before Kashi would be all his.

19

Kashi was beside herself with worry and grief. She was so stressed out and didn't know where to turn. She didn't know what to do or who to talk to. In the past two weeks, she hadn't made or returned any phone calls to Reuben. She had purposely avoided running into him on campus and her cell phone had been blowing up with text messages and voicemails from him, which all went unanswered. It's not that she didn't want to see him or talk to him but she was AFRAID. She knew that Reuben was upset and worried about her but for his own safety, as well as hers, she had no choice but to avoid him. Kashi felt it best to go on with her life with Logan and pretend that nothing ever happened between them. She was sure that if Reuben knew where she lived, he would have already shown up and the chaos would have been worst. She loved Reuben with all of her being but at this point Logan had proved to her what he was capable of. He was a dangerous man and she knew he would make good on his promises. He had told her that if she didn't break it off with Reuben that life would never be the same for her again. For two weeks straight, Kashi had tossed and turned every night, unable to sleep and imagining what might happen if she refused to give in. There seemed to be no way out of this miserable life that she had been

Imari Rogan

forced to choose, but she knew that it was the safest choice for everyone involved.

****

Reuben hadn't talked to Kashi, since the day she had been sick at home. He left what seemed like a ton of text messages and voicemails, all of which received no response. He knew that something was wrong but wasn't sure exactly what. Had Kashi changed her mind about him? Had she been thinking about the wonderful weekend they spent together that maybe wasn't so wonderful after all? Had he said or done something wrong? Had they made love too soon? Maybe she didn't love him after all. But that was impossible! She had pledged her love to him and it was so real!! Had Logan done something to her? The negative thoughts just kept bombarding him. As he sat on the edge of the couch, he buried his head in his hands and before he realized it, the tears began to fall. Reuben had never cried over any woman except his mom, when she was abused by his father and ended up in the hospital. He stood up and began to pace the floor. He wiped his eyes with the back of his hands. He forced himself to think. Suddenly his emotions went from despair to anger in a New York minute. Reality hit him like a ton of bricks! It was LOGAN!!! He knew in his heart that Logan was behind all of this! There was no way that Kashi would have cut him off so abruptly. Their love was too powerful for that. What had that bastard done?! He snatched his car keys from the coffee table and rushed towards the door. He needed answers and he needed them NOW!!!

Twenty minutes later, Reuben found himself driving into the parking lot of Monisha's complex. He sat in the car for a moment and then climbed the stairs to peer into the window of her apartment. The blinds were closed but the lights were on. He assumed Monisha was at home. He had no clue how she would react when she saw him but none of that mattered now. He was desperate for answers. Maybe this was a bad idea. He hardly knew Monisha and they had only met a couple of times. Before he could talk himself into leaving, Reuben paused for a moment before knocking twice on her door. He waited patiently as he heard movement from inside. Monisha opened the door with a look of shock, that quickly turned to fear. Reuben knew that he was the last person she expected to see but judging from the look, he knew she had the information that he wanted. "May I come in?" Monisha hesitated for a moment before finally stepping aside to let him in. "May I?" he asked, pointing to the living room sofa. Monisha nodded as Reuben took a seat. He buried his head in his hands, as he had been accustomed to doing these past few days. He let out a long sigh. Monisha took a seat across from him and waited for him to speak. "Monisha" he began, "I'm really sorry for popping up like this but I didn't know what else to do. I haven't talked to Kashi in two weeks. She hasn't returned any of my texts or phone calls. The last time that we spoke was the day after our trip, when she was at home sick with the flu. You're her best friend and I know that you know what's going on. I don't mean to pressure you or put you in the middle of all of this but I really need to know what's going on." Monisha felt a lump growing in her throat, as she struggled not to cry. Kashi had called her in hysterics after Logan had left her house with the photos, and explained to her everything that had happened including the blackmail. She was afraid for her life if she went against his wishes and she couldn't risk Reuben finding out for fear of hunting Logan down and them hurting each other. She had made Monisha swear not to say anything if Reuben ever showed up at her apartment. She figured that eventually that he would and she was right.

Monisha fought back tears as she finally spoke. "Kashi wants nothing to do with you. She doesn't want you anymore." "You're lying" he said. She ignored him. "I'm not lying but I can assure you that Kashi is done with you. It's over between the two of you, so may I suggest you continue with life as you know it." It was difficult for Monisha to keep direct eye contact with Reuben. She wasn't very good at telling lies but this was a necessary evil. Lives could be at stake. She did what she had to do and it hurt her to the core. "So that's it?" he asked, his voice cracking just barely above a whisper. "Yes, I'm sorry." Monisha stated matter of factly. Reuben dropped his head as he got up to leave. He didn't even bother making eye contact with her. "Don't bother seeing me out." Reuben walked to the door and silently closed it behind him. His legs felt like rubber, as he walked down the stairs to his car. He started the engine and glanced up at Monisha's apartment window. She was standing in the window staring at him as he left. As he drove off, he had no idea where he was headed. He had no direction, no vision, no anything. Life was suddenly on hold as he knew it.

Imari Rogan

20

Two months had passed and spring was almost gone. Summer would be moving in next month. Kashi still had not returned any of Reuben's phone calls and finally, he just stopped calling her altogether. In the meantime, Kashi had made the heart wrenching decision to return her engagement ring to Reuben. It wasn't fair to tie his life up with a false commitment and she decided that it was best for him to continue his life without her. Maybe he would find someone else. Someone who was more deserving of his love. He was going to make an excellent husband one day to a blessed and lucky woman. It was just too bad that it wouldn't be her. The night before she mailed the ring back, she cried herself to sleep. The next morning, she drove to the local post office with the ring securely sealed in a bubble manila envelope. She had carefully written Reuben's name and address on the envelope with no return address. She could only imagine the heartbreak and pain he would feel when he opened the package, but she had no choice. Over the next couple of weeks that led up to the end of classes, Kashi had purposely avoided running into Reuben on campus. She refused to have lunch in the cafeteria and left most of her classes about ten minutes early to avoid any contact. It worked. Reuben's college graduation came and went and

Kashi wasn't there. It was really officially over now. He had graduated. He was gone.

Kashi's parents were over the moon again. She had informed them that the wedding plans between her and Logan could continue. They were happy that she had finally come to her senses. Logan had become even more aggressive and confident in his behavior around Kashi because he knew that his devious and diabolical plan had worked. He now dropped by the condo whenever he felt like it, showering Kashi with expensive flowers and gifts trying to win her heart. Logan was truly in his element now. He was happy and elated. He didn't care anymore that Kashi wasn't truly happy. That her "love" was fake and coerced. Just as long as she belonged to him was all that mattered. He was selfish and he knew it but it felt too good to him to stop. She would now be his WIFE within the next six months and he was proud of himself for all he had accomplished. All of his schemes and dirty efforts had paid off. It would be HIM laying in bed with Kashi night after night. It would be HIM that would now penetrate Kashi like Reuben had and she was going to like it! He was on a mission to make Kashi LOVE him no matter what!

****

After Kashi's classes had ended, she became even more depressed. She had a choice to take summer classes but had decided against them because she was an emotional wreck. Reuben was gone and Logan was back. Her world and life had been flipped upside down and she almost hated everything and everyone in it. She hardly talked to anyone and her appetite had faded. She had frequent headaches and her stomach was always upset.

One night after dinner, her mother asked her what was wrong. "It's nothing mom, I just haven't been feeling well lately." She placed her hand on Kashi's forehead. "You're not running a fever." Kashi didn't reply. She just wanted to be left alone.

"It must be wedding jitters," her mother laughed but it wasn't funny to Kashi and in that very moment she felt rage. For for the first time in her life, she wanted to slap the living daylights out of her mother. Her stomach began to churn and she excused herself to her bedroom. She sat on the side of the bed and patiently tried to wait for the nausea to subside. It was no use. Kashi ran to the bathroom and barely made it to the toilet. She threw up all of her dinner. Oh my God what's wrong with me, she asked herself. She cleaned herself and returned to bed. She laid down for a moment and got lost in her thoughts. She missed Reuben! She was so stressed about her life that it was starting to make her sick.

All of a sudden, she sat straight up in bed as if someone had yanked her. Her eyes were wide with terror. She looked as if she had seen a ghost. She jumped out of bed and grabbed her datebook from her purse. She carefully and meticulously scanned the dates. She flipped back and forth between the last two to three months. Her last period had been the week before she spent the weekend with Reuben and she hadn't had one since. That was over two months ago.... nearly three! Oh my God, she thought. "I'm pregnant!" she said aloud. Feelings of joy and dread washed over her at once. Joy because she was carrying Reuben's child and dread because of what was going to happen once her parents and Logan found out. Kashi grabbed her cell phone and hurriedly called Monisha, who had barely answered when Kashi frantically whispered into the phone. "Monisha I'm in big trouble and I need to come over right away!!" "What's wrong Kashi?! "I'll explain later, I'll be there in a few!" Kashi hung up the phone and changed her clothes. She told her mother she would be right back and was going to visit Monisha for a while. "Okay, sweetheart be careful." her mom replied, as Kashi walked out of the door. By the time she arrived at Monisha's, Kashi was in tears and fell into Monisha's arms, as the door opened.

"Oh my goodness what's wrong?!! Kashi could barely catch her breath, as she made her way to the couch. She was choking on her sobs. Monisha just kept rubbing Kashi's back trying to get her to calm down. Kashi finally looked up at her through her tears. "Oh Monisha, I think I'm pregnant!! Monisha stared at her for a long moment before responding. "What?" was all she could manage to ask. "I think I'm pregnant! Kashi repeated. Monisha tried to make sense of everything. "How can you be so sure?" Kashi began to explain. "Well, lately I've been feeling really weird and I've had a lot of headaches, a loss of appetite and a bout of vomiting. At first, I just thought it was stress because of my breakup with Reuben and being back with Logan but then I just realized today that I've missed two periods!" Neither of them knew what to say. Monisha finally spoke first. "I have an extra pregnancy test in the bathroom, go and take it and we'll go from there." Kashi obediently nodded her head. She arose from the couch and headed towards the bathroom with Monisha close behind when Kashi suddenly stopped and turned to face her. "What are you doing with an "extra" pregnancy test? she asked, while raising an eyebrow. "For the same reason that you need one!" she answered. Both women broke into hysterical laughter. Monisha followed Kashi into the bathroom and handed her the pregnancy test from cabinet. "Read the instructions and come out when you're done." Monisha closed the door behind her and returned to the living room. She sat on the edge of the couch and thought about what would happen if Kashi was really pregnant. She tried to push the thought from her mind when Kashi returned to the living room, holding the test wand in her hand. Her hands were trembling when she handed the test to Monisha, who slowly looked at the results. Two red lines stared back at her. Kashi started crying all over again. Her friend was pregnant with Reuben's baby.

Imari Rogan

21

Reuben was barely existing and wasn't eating or sleeping very much. He had dropped about fifteen pounds from his regular 200 pound frame and it showed. It was one thing for Kashi to stop speaking to him but it was another thing altogether for her to return the engagement ring. He remembered the day he had gone to the mailbox to retrieve the mail, as was his daily routine. However, that day as he went to the mailbox, he felt different. He couldn't explain it. It was almost like an eerie premonition that he tried to brush away. Reuben reached into the mailbox and pulled out a stack of mail, but in the middle of the letters, magazines and junk mail, a brown manila envelope stood out. Reuben glanced at the familiar handwriting and his heart skipped a beat, as he went inside to open it. He had no idea what he would find. With no return address, he knew it was from Kashi. He opened it and pulled out layers of beautiful pink and purple tissue paper. As he opened the paper, he could faintly smell her signature perfume. Wrapped deep inside the layers was her engagement ring. There was no note, no letter and no explanation. Reuben felt a lump rise in his throat before the tears began to fall. He tucked the ring into his jeans pocket, threw the envelope in the trash and retreated to his bedroom. He closed the door where he could grieve in private. He sat down on the edge of his bed and allowed the sobs to overtake him. He was angry too. Why had she done this to them? He had so many questions that had gone unanswered. Whatever the reason, he knew that Logan was behind it all.

****

After his graduation ceremony, Reuben's parents gave him a huge after party at their home, complete with a private D.J and catered dinner. The party was festive but Reuben just sulked around and faked happiness with all of the guests. When his mom and sister asked him where Kashi was, he just made up an excuse. He was just too embarrassed to admit that she had broken up with him, but was determined that he was going to find out what was going on and win her back. She was everything to him. Kashi was his world.

In the days that followed, Reuben knew that he had to go on with his life, so he began applying for jobs at a few law firms. He got a few interviews and even a few offers, but quickly changed his mind. Kashi was his first priority right now and he needed to get to the bottom of things before he committed to a career. He knew that it may not be the wisest choice but right now he didn't care. He needed to concentrate on what mattered the most to him. He simply wasn't willing to let the love of his life slip away without a fight. He decided to get radical. His plan was to somehow track Logan down and find out what was going on. He knew he could be placing himself in a potentially dangerous situation but at this point he could have cared less. He began to browse the internet. He only knew of Logan's first name, so he googled the first name and the city and state. Absolutely nothing came up except for a couple of local businesses and eateries. This had to be a joke. What was his last name? Had Kashi ever mentioned it? He thought long and hard.

Finally he remembered. ROY!! Logan's last name was Roy, and he remembered Kashi mentioning that he was some type of doctor... Doctor Logan Roy.

Reuben typed his full name into the search engine and luckily only one result appeared. Reuben clicked on the link and lo and behold, the image that stared back at him was none other than Logan. The same guy from the movie theater. Not a bad looking guy but Reuben felt as if he was the best looking of the two. He smiled and forced himself to concentrate. Logan's office address, phone number and hospital that he worked at was mentioned underneath his picture.

A few more links revealed his *personal* address, home telephone number and personal cell number. Reuben had struck a goldmine. This was wonderful news. News that he would use. He printed out the information and tucked it safely away in his planner. He printed out two extra copies and placed them in his desk drawer. He leaned back in his desk chair feeling elated. He had all of the information that he needed. How he would use it was the next concern.

****

It was Saturday Night and Logan had already made plans for the evening. He would pick Kashi up and they would head downtown to a broadway play that was in town from New York City. The play had been sold out for weeks but Logan had managed to get VIP tickets for the last night's performance. They were also meeting with some of his colleagues and their wives in the private VIP section of the theater for dinner and cocktails. Logan was so happy that he was finally going to be able to show Kashi off to his colleagues, who had been asking about her. Logan talked about her all of the time and they were beginning to wonder if Kashi was a real person or a figment of Logan's imagination.

As Logan climbed out of the shower, he heard the landline phone ringing in the other room. He grabbed a towel and rushed to answer it thinking that it may be Kashi or his on call service. He quickly glanced at the caller ID. The number was unavailable. "Hello?" he answered out of breath. CLICK. He thought nothing of it. He padded to his bedroom closet and quickly dressed. He chose a black tuxedo with a white shirt bow tie and black alligator shoes. It was strictly a black tie affair and he had asked Kashi to dress accordingly. He splashed on his favorite cologne, grabbed the tickets from the dresser and headed out the door.

When he arrived to pick up Kashi to his amazement she was wearing the exact opposite of what he had asked her to wear. Instead of a black formal gown, she was wearing a short red sequined dress with red high heeled shoes. She was still beautiful nonetheless but Logan was furious that she had defied his wishes.

He escorted her in silence to the car and once they were inside he asked her what was wrong. "Nothing!" she retorted. "Well why didn't you wear the dress that I asked you to wear?" "Because I didn't want to you asshole!" "Whoa!" Where did that attitude come from? he wondered.

Logan decided to ignore Kashi and instead make light conversation. He didn't want her to embarrass him tonight in front of his friends, so he tried to reach her good side. "You smell really good Kashi, what's the name of the fragrance you're wearing? "RAID!! she hissed. She wanted to laugh at her own joke but she was so angry right now that she didn't dare. Logan was hurt and he had a feeling that the rest of the evening wasn't going to be pleasant.

****

Brief introductions were made before the play started and Kashi merely nodded her head in everyone's direction and barely smiled. It was obvious to everyone present that she was not happy to be there. Their seats were located in the VIP section on the first floor, near the side of the stage. Private waiters catered to their every need, serving drinks, hors d'oeuvres and dinner. But Kashi was miserable and she was making Logan miserable. She barely ate anything and just picked over her food. She didn't feel well and wished that she had stayed at home.

Finally the lights dimmed and the play started. As the room darkened, Kashi felt relieved because she no longer had to face Logan. He disgusted her. She tried to concentrate on the show but her stomach kept turning. She felt so sick. She reached for her glass of soda on the table in front of her hoping a few sips would be soothing. She was about to excuse herself and go to the ladies room when suddenly the theatre lights came back on; it was intermission. Logan turned to face her and reached for her hand. She snatched it away. His face turned red with anger because some of his colleagues were watching.

He leaned over and whispered in her ear, "BEHAVE!" He leaned back in his chair and reached for her hand again. This time she didn't snatch away, but he was squeezing her hand pretty hard and it hurt. She hated him and was furious with him. How dare he speak to her as if she was a child. Behave huh? Okay, if he wanted to treat her like a child, she was going to act like one. She wanted to shame him in the worst way and now was her opportunity. The wave of nausea only worsened and instead of her rushing to get up and go to the ladies room, she purposely turned her head to throw up on the floor in front of everyone. She heaved and gagged until she was finished. The wives of his colleagues rushed to Kashi's side with napkins and paper towels and led her outside to the ladies room. On her way, she glanced back over her shoulder at Logan, who looked absolutely mortified . She felt better for that and so did her tummy. She was laughing so hard on the inside!

Once in the ladies room, she assured everyone that she was okay. She rinsed her mouth and washed her hands at the sink. She thanked all of the ladies for their kindness before excusing herself into a stall. She breathed a sigh of relief and waited for the ladies to leave. She stepped out and glanced sideways at herself in the mirror. She ran her hand across her belly and smiled. A part of Reuben was growing inside of her but she wasn't showing. At least not yet. She had no idea what the future would hold but she already knew in her heart that she was going to keep their baby.

****

The argument started once they were seated in the car. "How dare you embarrass me the way that you did tonight! What in the hell is wrong with you?" Logan screamed. Kashi refused to respond. She simply looked at him. She was so happy inwardly. She was glad she had embarrassed him. He deserved it. "ANSWER ME!!" he screamed. "I threw up" she replied, looking him square in his eyes. He raised his hand to slap her but quickly withdrew it. "That's right, you'd better not hit me again because if you do, I'll try to kill you!" She peered at him through squinted eyes and she meant every word that she spoke. All of a sudden his whole demeanor changed. He went from rage to compassion seemingly instantly. "Kashi?" he asked. "What's the matter with you? I know that you embarrassed me on purpose tonight. I'm not stupid and I know that you hate me, but try to love me because I love you so much and I want you to be happy." His eyes filled with tears and his voice cracked as he talked. "If you want me to be happy Logan, then leave me alone!" Logan glared at her before starting the car and burning rubber away from the curb. He sped down the side streets of downtown until he reached the freeway. He drove at 85 miles per hour. Kashi was so scared that they would have an accident, as he bobbed and weaved through traffic like a madman. His eyes were raging with anger and she was absolutely sure they would be killed that night. He cut off a truck and than slammed on his brakes to avoid hitting a car front of them, which caused the truck to swerve into the next lane. Despite what had just happened, Logan continued with his reckless driving. Kashi silently prayed they would get pulled over by the police but they didn't. She gripped the door handle for dear life until they miraculously arrived in front of her condo. "Here we are my love." he sang happily with a smile. Kashi was terrified and shaking. Logan needed help in the worst way. Somehow she managed to quickly climb out of the car and half walked and ran to the door entrance. God please help me, she cried inwardly. Please help us all!

22

Kashi was starting to gain weight. In the weeks that had passed, her clothes were starting to fit really tight. She could no longer button her jeans and her breasts were sore and enlarged. With summer's arrival, Kashi wasn't going to be able to hide underneath baggy jackets and sweatshirts much longer. She needed to go shopping pronto. She had to hide this pregnancy for as long as possible. She called Monisha and asked her to take her shopping. It was the weekend and it was blazing hot outside. The news said that the temperature was 90 degrees and slowly climbing. It could reach as high as 100.

Kashi didn't know what she was going to wear to the mall. Her choices were definitely limited. She rummaged through her closet and managed to find an old pair of jeans and a baggy t-shirt. She was forced to leave the jeans unzipped but luckily the t-shirt covered it. "How are you feeling today?" Monisha asked, once Kashi was seated in the car. "Much better, the morning sickness has subsided since I'm approaching the second trimester. Can you tell that I'm pregnant?" "Yes, but it's only because I know that you are. Your face is a little bit fuller but that's all." "Well thank God I'm getting new clothes today. I'm not taking any chances on anyone finding out too soon"

Imari Rogan

Once they arrived at the mall, Kashi made her way to the main department store. As Monisha was helping her pick out clothing, Kashi felt that all too familiar feeling again. She felt as if someone was watching her. She quickly glanced around and didn't see anyone, so she continued adding clothes to the basket. When she was satisfied with the items she had picked out, they made their way down the main aisle towards the fitting room. That's when Kashi noticed a familiar face moving towards them in the opposite direction. Her heart skipped a beat when she recognized who it was. It was Reuben. She quickly turned the cart around and began walking in the opposite direction. "What's wrong with you?!" Monisha asked, while trying to maneuver the cart. "I just saw Reuben coming towards us. Didn't you see him?" "NO! I didn't! Monisha responded, while looking back over her shoulder. "Don't look back! Kashi demanded but it was too late. Reuben had already seen them. Both women tried to duck down a different aisle but it was no use. He caught up to them and approached them from behind. "Kashi? Monisha? What are you guys doing here?" Kashi felt her legs go weak beneath her and the sound of his voice snatched her breath away. She slowly turned to face him and when she did, she broke into tears. Reuben quickly took her into his arms. She buried her face in his chest and cried.

Monisha didn't know what to do, so she silently excused herself. "I'll see you by the fitting rooms Kashi" she said, as she walked away. Reuben continued to hold Kashi. "I know that you still love me sweetheart, I know that you love me, and I love you too. I'll never stop loving you," he whispered in her ear, as they stood in the middle of the aisle. Shoppers were forced to walk around them, as they stood there holding each other. Time stood still. Reuben had waited three long and lonely months to hold her again and he didn't care who had a problem with it. He stroked her back and held her tight. When she was finally able to look at him, she told him everything that he needed to hear. "I love you so much!" Reuben's eyes filled with tears and he bit his lip to keep the tears from falling. "Stay right here" Kashi whispered. "I'll be right back." She took the shopping cart to the fitting rooms where Monisha had taken a seat and was patiently waiting. "I'm going to go and talk to Reuben, so give us a few minutes." Monisha nodded her head as Kashi walked away.

Reuben led Kashi outside to the car and when they were seated inside, he turned the engine on and started the air conditioning. He looked her square in the eyes. "So what happened to us?" he asked. "Logan" she said simply. "I thought so." Reuben allowed her to continue. "The day that I last spoke with you, the day that I had the flu, Logan showed up at my door shortly after that and blackmailed me. He had an envelope full of pictures of us that were taken at the cabin but they weren't just any pictures. They were pictures of us making love." She watched his eyes widen with disbelief and his jaw tighten with anger but he didn't interrupt her. Kashi continued. "He hired a private detective to follow us, so that he could blackmail me into marrying him. He said that he would show the pictures to our parents and family if I refused to oblige with his wishes. He said my reputation would be ruined and that my family would disown me. He also said that he would make my life miserable If I didn't go along with things. He told me to break it off with you and I was afraid not to, so that's why I didn't return any of your phone calls and I returned the ring to you. It was Logan who made all of the prank calls, slashed my tire and broke out your car window."

When she had finished, Reuben sat in stunned silence. He stared straight ahead as he shook his head from side to side. "There's more" she whispered. He turned to face her. "I'm pregnant...three months to be exact." Reuben reached out to her and hugged her. Now it was his turn to cry. "Oh my God Kashi, are you serious? A part of me is growing inside of you?" "Yes, Reuben, I'm carrying your child, our child and it feels so amazing." They held each for a long time. "Where do we go from here?" he finally asked. "I don't know" Kashi said, "I'm hoping that you might have an idea." "Well, I do know for sure that lunatic Logan will NOT be raising our child. There is no way I will ever allow that to happen. How does he think that he's going to marry you and you're pregnant with someone else's baby?" "Well, he doesn't know yet. No one knows except for you and Monisha." Reuben sighed heavily, while thinking what their next move should be.

Finally, he spoke. "If you marry Logan to save your reputation and keep your parent's respect, then you'll live a miserable life for the rest of your life. You can't lie about the child being his because it's mine and I'm clearly not Indian. This child will draw a wedge between everyone anyway. With that being the case, I don't think that you have any choice except to tell everyone the truth. It's time for you to live your life for you and you deserve to be happy. Your life shouldn't be fabricated with someone that you don't love. Our baby is meant to be and as quiet as it's kept, I think that he or she has already made the decision for you." Kashi stared at her lap for a moment before responding. "You're absolutely right. I refuse to live my life through my parent's eyes. I can't and I won't. Pregnant or not. I want to be with you and only you and I want to be your

Imari Rogan

wife for life and I'm willing to risk everything to take that chance."

Reuben was speechless. He was so grateful that she still loved him and wanted to be his wife. He was in awe of her. It was Kashi who spoke again. "Will you do me a huge favor?" "Yes, anything" "Give me some time to break the news to Logan and my family. I'm going to try and hide the pregnancy long enough to make an exit plan. Maybe I can move in with Monisha or something, because I know my parents are going to throw me out." "Don't worry about that. You can move in with me at my parent's house or we can get an apartment together but you can best believe that you won't be out on the street with nowhere to go."

"Thank you so much Reuben. I really appreciate and love you for stepping into the middle of all of this nonsense but one day I'm sure it will all be worth it. In the meantime, I'll continue to lay low and I promise to keep you posted.

I'd better get back to Monisha in the dressing room, so I can try on my new clothes for my growing belly." Kashi smiled. Reuben lifted her shirt and planted a kiss on her very small but slowly growing baby bump. He then moved to her forehead and kissed it too. "I'll be in touch" Kashi said, as she got out of the car. When she returned to the dressing room, she explained everything to Monisha including her plan to tell Logan about the baby. Monisha looked scared . "Kashi please don't do that!" she begged. "Logan may try to kill the both of you!" "Well, let him try and he just may end up dead himself" she countered. "I just hope that you know what you're doing!" "Do you have any other suggestions?" Kashi asked, while looking Monisha directly in her eyes. "No, I don't" she answered, dropping her head. "Well, everyone will know the truth sooner or later". "Kashi I'm just afraid for you." "Don't be" Kashi answered, while trying to keep her voice calm. "Everything will work out, I'm confident that it will" but Kashi didn't sound too convincing…..especially to herself.

23

Logan hadn't seen Kashi since the night of the play, which was about three weeks earlier. Surprisingly, he had decided that they needed some time away from each other. Once again, he had allowed his anger to get the best of him and after the wild ride on the freeway, he was somewhat ashamed of himself. He considered it lucky that he hadn't killed them both. Logan had called Kashi a couple of times afterwards to apologize but she had only hung up on him. Kashi didn't want to talk to him. What was wrong with him? Why did his anger always get the best of him? Why did he always react the opposite of his good intentions?

He thought for a long hard moment. Maybe he needed counseling. Maybe he needed to see a good psychotherapist but he didn't want to ruin his reputation either. The doctor needing a doctor? He chuckled at the thought. He ran his hands through his already muffled hair and stared at the floor. Kashi Kashi Kashi! He was crazy for her. He thought back to the forbidden night once again and felt his manhood rise. He wanted her this very moment. Just as Logan reached for himself, his phone rang. He silently cursed under his breath and went into the kitchen to answer it. "Hello?" CLICK. He placed the phone back on the base. Who kept calling him and hanging up?

The hang ups had become more frequent during the last couple of weeks. The caller ID kept displaying "Blocked Call." He was beginning to get agitated.

Logan returned to the living room couch and began thinking about the strange calls. He remembered that he had been getting a few calls at the office too that were hang ups. Maybe he had pissed off one of his patients, who had randomly gotten a hold of his personal landline phone but that was strange because no one had made any complaints against him. As a matter of a fact, his patient list was only growing in numbers and his appointments were always booked, so that couldn't be it. Somewhat irritated he decided to shower and go to the office. He needed to be in a different environment for some peace and quiet and his apartment just wasn't the place for that.

It was Saturday and the office was closed, so he decided that he would take advantage of the solitude and catch up on some files at the same time. Logan left his apartment and when he reached his car, he noticed that something was amiss. It was nothing that was too obvious but something was off. He glanced at his car. Yes, there it was. It looked as if someone had tried to break into it on the driver's side with some type of object. The door handle was scratched and had a little dent on it. Some of the paint was missing as well, just underneath the lock. As Logan ran his fingers over the paint, he tried to buff the scratch out. When that didn't work, he decided it was best to let a body shop do the repairs. He let out a disgusted sigh, opened the car door and got in. He checked the front and back seats, the dashboard and the steering column. Everything seemed to be intact. It had probably been a would be car thief that got spooked away. He started up the engine and drove to his office. His thoughts returned to Kashi. He missed her and wanted to see her. He decided he would call her tonight and make a dinner date. Just the thought of seeing her again lifted his mood and by the time that he reached his office building, he was almost smiling. He punched in the code to the alarm system and let himself in. He walked down the narrow dimly lit hallway to the elevators and pressed the button. He got off on the third floor and walked down the hall to his office suite. After unlocking the door, Logan had to collect all the mail off of the floor, that had accumulated through the door slot. He walked into his office, flipped on the light and began to sort through the mail.

When he reached the bottom of the pile, he noticed a large envelope. It contained his name but didn't have a return address. He tossed it to the side, gathered the rest of the mail and distributed it among his colleague's offices. When he returned to his office, he sat down and picked up the strange envelope from the desk. He carefully tore it open and read the letter that had been typed in bold red ink. 'HELLO DR. ROY. I HOPE YOU'RE ENJOYING YOUR DAY THUS FAR. I REALLY DON'T WANT TO SPOIL THE SURPRISE, BUT THIS LETTER SERVES AS A REMINDER THAT I AM NOT PLEASED WITH YOU. IN THE FUTURE YOU NEED TO BE A LITTLE MORE CAREFUL.

The letter wasn't signed. Logan frowned as he read the letter again. Who had sent it? A disgruntled patient? Possibly, but what had he done? Once again, he hadn't received any complaints. Was it someone who sat on the medical board that had a problem with him? That was a possibility too but it would have been nice to know what he had done wrong in the first place. Logan shook his head from side to side in confusion and attempted to get some work done. He caught up on a few patient files and dictated a few memos into his recorder for his medical transcriptionist the following week. He wanted to get more work done but the strange letter left him feeling quite uneasy. After a couple of hours, he decided to call it a day and packed up to leave. When he reached the empty parking lot, the sun was already starting to set. He couldn't help looking over his shoulder as he got into his car and drove off. Now the tables were turned and he was the one feeling paranoid.

****

Reuben was pleased and patted himself on the back for all of the hang up calls he had made to Logan's residence. He had even made a few to his office phone as well, to really make things look suspicious. The letter that he dropped off after office hours was really the icing on the cake. Reuben had sat in his Range Rover in the shadows of the office parking lot and waited for the medical staff to leave, before he entered the building. He had hurriedly rushed up to the third floor and dropped the letter in the mail slot. The cleaning crew were the only people, who had remained in the building and they were none the wiser. Reuben wanted Logan to know how it felt to be on the receiving end of stalking. Since Logan was a doctor, it would be a little more difficult to figure out who the culprit was. Logan needed a dose of his own medicine and Reuben was going to make sure he choked on it.

24

Logan had been utterly distracted with the hang ups and the letters that had continued to plague him. The letters weren't only coming to his office but now they were being delivered to his apartment too. Whoever was doing this, was pretty smart because the letters weren't being delivered through the postal service. Someone was placing the letters directly into his mailbox, so it was impossible to trace them via a postmark. Each letter was becoming more threatening than the previous ones. They contained such threats as: I'M WATCHING YOU or BE VERY CAREFUL WHERE YOU GO AT NIGHT! Logan was so uneasy that he began to ask his neighbors if they had seen anyone suspicious lurking around his mailbox but everyone assured him they had not. It only made matters worse that the apartment building didn't have any security cameras. Every move that he made was with caution and fear. He didn't know what this person was capable of.

It wasn't until almost the end of July that Logan and Kashi finally touched base. She was glad that they hadn't seen each other for a while because it gave her time to think and get up her nerve to call the relationship off. She had called him at his office one afternoon and told him that she needed to see him. Even though Logan was booked solid with patients, he assigned them to his physician's assistant and promptly left. Whenever Kashi summoned for him, he answered promptly. Her wishes were his demands and he was going to see to it that every wish she made was met.

Kashi asked Logan to come to the condo, so they could talk. She was finally going to break up with him once and for all and watch him go insane. Her parents were working overtime with patients and the twins were staying with relatives for the summer, so there was no excuse to prolong the inevitable. As she waited for him to arrive, she paced the living room floor. Now she had regrets about asking to see him. She reached for her cell phone and called Reuben. She told him that Logan was on his way and that she was going to break up with him. "I think I need to be there" "No Reuben, you can't" "Why not?" "Because you guys may start fighting and I don't have the strength or the means to break up a fight between two grown men."

"Well, I don't want him to hurt you and that's all I'm really concerned about. After watching my mom get abused, I'm not going to stand around and watch the love of my life and the mother of my unborn child go through the same thing!" Kashi regretted calling him. He sounded so angry and defensive. "Reuben please," she begged. She wasn't able to think of anything else to say. " Okay, give me the address I'm on my way! "Reuben No!" Kashi yelled. "Please think about me and the baby. What will I do if you guys get into a fight? I'm helpless to do anything." Reuben let out a long sigh and thought for a moment. "Okay" he finally agreed. "I'm still going to come but I can park across the street from your condo and wait until Logan arrives. I want you to place me on speaker phone, so I can hear everything that's going on. If he gets violent, I'm breaking the door down and I'm killing that motherfucker do you understand me?" Kashi didn't have any choice but to agree. "Okay" she finally said. She gave him her address. "I'm on my way."

Reuben arrived first, and parked on the opposite side of the street but down a little ways, so he wouldn't be so obvious. He made sure that he could still see the front entrance of Kashi's condo. He waited impatiently for Logan to arrive. After about ten minutes, he finally saw the sleek black Mercedes Benz, with the tinted black windows, drive into the driveway. Reuben called Kashi and told her that Logan had arrived. He reminded her to place him on speaker phone. Kashi did as she was asked and Reuben placed his phone on mute, to cancel any possible background noises.

When Kashi met Logan at the front door, he pulled her into his arms. "I missed you so much" he breathed. Kashi tried to break free from his embrace but he was too strong for her. She kept her arms at her sides and refused to return his embrace. He finally let go and she led him into the living room and gestured for him to sit down across from her. He ignored her and sat next to her instead. Kashi's cell phone was tucked safely away in the pocket of her sundress and she hoped that Reuben could hear everything. "It's been a long time since we've seen each other and I'm glad that you called me. What is it you'd like to talk about?" Logan asked. "Us, living this lie", Kashi stated, as she looked straight at him as she spoke.

"Well that's just wonderful," he yelled, as he got up from where he was seated. He started pacing the floor. "Here we go again! You call me off from work and drag me over here only to tell me once again about the so called "lie" we're living. How many times do I have to tell you WHAT we are GOING to do and HOW we are going to do it?! You are going to marry me and that's all there is to it! DO YOU UNDERSTAND ME?" Logan was standing over her with rage in his eyes and his face was red with anger. "Logan, you need to calm down. The way you're behaving right now is a very good indicator of how you'll respond after we're married and that's one of the reasons I'm terrified to be with you."

Logan furiously ran his hands through his hair and sat back down on the couch beside her. "I'm sorry" he said softly. Kashi was amazed that his temperament could go from rage to compassion so quickly. It was like he had two different personalities.

"Let me get you something to drink," she said, quickly rising from the couch and heading towards the kitchen. She needed to get away from him for a moment. She thought about what she was going to say next. She heard his footsteps directly behind her. Why couldn't he just stay where he was? She ignored him and went to the refrigerator and opened the door. She peered nervously inside and grabbed the pitcher of lemonade . When she closed the door and turned around, Logan was standing directly in front of her. She could feel his breath on her face. His eyes were full of suspicion. "Wait a minute" he said, while stepping back from her. He looked at her as if seeing her for the first time. "You've gained a little bit of weight, since I last saw you." It was more of question than a statement. Kashi felt her legs start to tremble. She strategically held the pitcher of lemonade in front of her stomach. "Your face is a little fuller too but the extra weight looks good on you."

Logan moved to the side to allow Kashi to grab two glasses from the kitchen cabinet. She breathed a sigh of relief that he hadn't noticed her growing belly, hidden beneath her sundress. As she stood beside the kitchen sink drinking her lemonade, Logan approached her and pulled her into his arms. This time it was a little bit closer than before. "Kiss me!" he demanded. Kashi placed her glass on the counter as Logan forced his tongue into her mouth. All of a sudden, he let her go.

Logan looked at Kashi, as if he had seen a ghost. His eyes grew wide, as he slowly moved back and placed his hand on her belly. Now it was Kashi's eyes that grew big. He must have felt her belly when he had pulled her close to him.

"What's this?" he asked in shock. "What's going on? Are you PREGNANT?" Kashi watched as his eyes filled with tears. "Yes" she whispered. "Oh my God, oh my God" Logan yelled, as he began to sob uncontrollably. He stumbled slightly backwards and slumped over the kitchen counter. He buried his face in his hands and cried and cried. Kashi watched in despair. She could only imagine how he must be feeling, but at least now he knew. She watched as he pulled some napkins out of his trousers and pitifully dabbed at his eyes. He left the kitchen and returned to the living room. Kashi could hear him wailing like a baby. She went into the living room and sat down beside him. He still had his face buried in his hands and his shoulders shook. He finally faced her. His eyes were bloodshot.

"Reuben's baby?" he asked. Kashi nodded her head yes.

Logan's voice was strangely calm when he responded. "Kashi, I'm so disappointed in you. Sleeping with that nigger is one thing, but getting pregnant is altogether different. You're a pathetic little slut who doesn't even deserve the type of life that I was willing to share with you. Life as you now know it, is going to change forever. I will see to it that our families are informed in the worst way of the disgraceful act that you have committed. You will be exposed once I show everyone the photos of you and Reuben, in the throes of passion. Every ounce of respect for you will forever be lost from this point on. You are a disgrace to our Indian heritage and I'm almost sorry that I ever met you."

Logan silently arose from the couch and walked to the front door. He calmly opened it and let himself out. He never looked back. Not for a second did he notice Reuben sitting in his car across the street, waiting to come to Kashi's defense if necessary.

25

"How could you do this to us?" her mother wailed, as Kashi walked through the front door. Kashi was returning from the mall with Monisha and she was tired and hot. They had met at the mall to get out of the house and talk. Kashi brought Monisha up to speed about everything that happened in the last few weeks, including the breakup with Logan. Kashi was bracing herself for the worse not knowing when she returned home, the worst was already waiting for her. She did think it was strange that both of her parent's cars were home in the middle of the day. They were supposed to be working but then she noticed Logan's car too. She braced herself for the inevitable.

As Kashi entered the living room, her mother was crying silently, as tears streaked her mascara. "How could you do this to us?" her mom asked again. Logan was seated next to his parents on the living room couch and her father was seated on the love seat. Mr. and Mrs. Roy were also wiping away tears, while Logan showed no remorse.

"Did you hear me?" her mother repeated. "I asked you how could you do this to us?' Kashi sat down in the corner of the room and took a deep breath before responding. She wanted to know how much information had been revealed to them. "Do what?" she asked. Her father arose from his seat and stood over her with clenched teeth. She thought he was going to hit her. Between clenched teeth he spoke. "Betray Logan and this entire family by sleeping with someone, who we know absolutely nothing about and then having the nerve to get pregnant!" Kashi's eyes met Logan's. She hated him and it showed. She swallowed her tears. "How do you know that any of this is true?" she asked. Kashi's mother snatched the manila envelope from the coffee table. She reached inside the envelope and threw the pictures at Kashi's face. The photos hit Kashi on the forehead and landed on the floor facing upwards for everyone to view again.

Mr. and Mrs. Roy grimaced at the images they were forced to look at, while turning their heads away in disgust. It was Kashi's father who spoke again after everyone had regained their composure. "We will not tolerate this kind of behavior and we refuse to be disgraced. I speak for everyone in this room when I say that you WILL TERMINATE the pregnancy and follow through with your plans for this marriage. Is that understood?! If you don't, then we want nothing more to do with you!" Her father continued to stand over her in disgust. Kashi couldn't believe what she was hearing. Were they asking her to abort her baby? Were they asking her to abort their grandchild? "Mom and dad please calm down and have a seat, I have something that I need to say." Surprisingly, they did as they were asked.

Kashi stood up and moved to the middle of the room to face her family, Logan's family and Logan. The people who were once family, were now her accusers and her enemies. With every bit of courage that she could glean on, she finally spoke. She addressed her mother and father first.

"As you know mom and dad and have known from the very beginning that I don't love Logan. I never have and I never will. I tried to love him but love is not something that can be fabricated. I know that you are firm believers in tradition and tradition believes that two people can grow to love each other even when they don't in the beginning. But it's been two years since I've dated Logan and my feelings have remained the same. There have been hundreds and thousands of couples down through the years, who have been forced into arraigned marriages to please family members, because no one wants to lose the respect and honor from their families. But after all is said and done, there are many couples that have lived miserable lives. I for one refuse to do that. I have begged and pleaded with both of you to please try and understand my feelings and my point of view but both of you have refused. You both consistently turned deaf ears to my concerns. As fate would have it, I met someone on my college campus one day and I didn't plan for it to happen. His name is Reuben and while we are both from very different cultures and worlds, we fell in love. We spent one beautiful weekend together and yes it was BEAUTIFUL at his family's private cottage and there we pledged our love to each other. Unbeknown to me, Logan had hired a private detective to follow my every move because he became suspicious after I broke up with him the first time. I think he had a feeling that I was seeing someone else and to find out for sure, he hired a detective. In the meantime my tires have been slashed, Reuben's car was keyed and his windows were broken out, while we were at the cabin and I know that Logan was behind all of it." She paused long enough to glare in Logan's direction and dared him with her eyes to deny it. She continued. "Also, you need to know that Logan has been very abusive to me. He violently slapped me across my face a few months ago while on a date, just because he was jealous and suspicious. But when I told you about it, you justified his behavior not to mention the countless other times he has physically manhandled me, whenever he gets angry and believe me, that's all the time. Logan is not the type of person that I would marry anyway and if you really loved me, you wouldn't dare ask me to abort my baby, your grandchild, just to save your reputation. That's selfish and I won't do it!"

The silence that followed, hung in the room like a dark cloud. Kashi's parents looked so sad. Kashi turned to face Logan's parents. "Mr. and Mrs. Roy, I have always loved and respected you. I don't believe that the lunatic actions of your son in anyway reflect you. I understand you did your best to raise him and want nothing but the best for him and for the most part, he turned out to be a very successful man, but Logan desperately needs psychiatric care. I have never been more afraid of anyone in my life except him. I will not live my life with someone that I am afraid of. Someone who is deranged and out of touch with reality. I'm not in love your son. He knows it. Everyone knows it. I have to follow my heart no matter the price I pay. I'm sorry".

They shook their heads in silence. They had no idea of what they were hearing or of the awful acts their son had committed. Kashi turned to Logan last. "Logan I wish nothing but the best for you in the future, wherever it leads you. I apologize that I wasn't able to love you the way that you wanted to be loved. My only desire is to live my life and be happy with someone who I love and loves me in return. Someone who respects me. I've found that with Reuben, so please just let us be. I'm afraid of you because of all the horrible things you've done and said to me all in the name of "love," Just so you know, I'll be seeking a personal protection order against you, as soon as possible. You need serious help and I hope you find it not only for your sake but for the sake of your family and friends. I truly hope that one day, you'll find that special someone who will love you with all of their heart."

Kashi turned and left the room. She left everyone sitting there lost in each of their thoughts. She hoped and prayed that they would understand and accept the choice she had chosen, because at the end of the day, it wasn't Kashi who was selfish, it was tradition.

26

As Kashi stood on the deck of the condo looking out into the evening sky, she thought about all of the events that had transpired over the last four months. As the chill of the November night air whipped around stirring her legs and tickling her face, she tried to wrap her arms around her belly for warmth. But that was a difficult task with her bulging belly. The baby was due next month and Kashi and Reuben planned to be married right after the baby's birth. She had one more year of college left but decided that she would finish once the baby had turned one. The night was peaceful and serene and except for the occasional baby kick, all seemed to be well despite the circumstances.

As tradition would dictate, her family had disowned her. The so called shame that she had exposed them to had been too great for them to overcome. Both families had been unforgiving and just as Kashi had expected, her parents asked her to move out. They questioned and harassed her relentlessly about her decision to date outside of her race. They wanted to know how and why God forbid, she chose to be with an African American? She didn't realize that the two people in the world, who had given her life and were supposed to love her unconditionally, would abandon her. However, Kashi was thankful that

Reuben had planned ahead and rented a condo for them as soon as he found out about the pregnancy. Things were looking up for Reuben as well. He had taken a job with his father's firm and was seeking to make partner in the near future. Kashi had not heard from Logan, since the night of the family meeting but she had gone to the police station the following day and filed a restraining order as promised. She wasn't going to take any chances whatsoever, for Logan to bring any future trouble in her life.

Kashi was so lost in her thoughts, that she jumped slightly when she felt a pair of arms embrace her from behind. She shifted her body sideways and snuggled into Reuben's arms. "I love you" he whispered. "I love you too." "Let's go inside, it's too cold out here for you and the baby". She followed Reuben into the family room and closed the patio doors behind them. They had dinner reservations for 7:00 and Kashi could hardly wait. She was so hungry. Within the last couple of weeks, she had been eating everything in sight. Reuben constantly laughed at the way she waddled around the house. She showered and changed her clothes and met Reuben in the living room. He carefully led her to the car and helped her inside. She chuckled to herself. He was so over protective of her, especially within these last few weeks. Reuben waited on her hand and foot and she had to admit that she was enjoying it.

Kashi could hardly wait for the waiter to bring them their food and dove into it like she had never eaten before. "Whoa girl, slow down it's not going anywhere."

Reuben laughed. She just waved her fork at him and ignored him. She was way too hungry for jokes. Kashi was halfway done with her meal, when all of a sudden she stopped eating. She placed her fork on the table and sat still for a moment. There it was again. That spooky feeling that they were being watched.

Reuben looked up from his plate and saw her staring into space. "Kashi what's wrong? Aren't you feeling well, is it the baby?" He looked worried. "No no, it's nothing like that," she assured him. "Then what's going on. What's wrong?"

Kashi glanced over her shoulder in both directions before answering. "I just have the feeling that we're being watched. The same feeling that I had when we were at the cabin and Logan was stalking us."

Reuben let out a long sigh before responding. "Kashi, please don't worry about that happening again. Logan is crazy but I don't think he's that crazy. There is no way that he would violate that restraining order. He's not allowed to come within 30 feet of us without risk of losing everything that he's worked for. He doesn't want to go to jail." Kashi thought about what Reuben said. "Maybe you're right" she agreed. He reached across the table and held her hand to reassure her.

"Hey, I have an idea," as he tried to redirect her thoughts to something positive. "What?" "After we leave here, let's go down to the lake's edge and take a short walk I have some blankets in the car and we can wrap up in them and take a nice walk before heading home" He watched her face light up. "That sounds wonderful! She was thankful that Reuben was in her life. He always knew exactly what to do and say even in her worst moments. By the time they reached the lake, she had forgotten all about the eerie feeling that she had earlier. Life was for living and she intended to live it to the fullest and not allow her fears to get the best of her.

27

As they walked hand in hand near the edge of the lake, life seemed almost perfect. The night was dark and the moonlight was all they needed, as they made their way through the sand.

The beach was deserted and the Range Rover was parked by itself a few feet behind them.

"Enjoying yourself?" Reuben asked. "Absolutely. Whenever I'm with you, I always enjoy myself." They stopped to kiss and their tongues intermingled with each other, as his hands moved to her backside. The warmth of their bodies underneath the blankets made the November air feel like Spring. Reuben wished they could make love right then and there but knew that wasn't possible. There was too much between them, so to speak. He chuckled inwardly and broke the embrace. They continued walking. After a few minutes, they decided to return to the car. As they headed back, Kashi felt that feeling again but decided to keep quiet. That's when she noticed a figure walking towards them coming from the wooded area. It was somewhat difficult to see exactly who it was because of the darkness. "Who is that?" she whispered to Reuben, as the figure slowly approached and stopped a few feet in front of them. She tightened her grip on Reuben's hand and began to tremble.

Kashi and Rueben froze in their tracks, as Logan moved closer and stood to face them. He was now only inches away.

It was Reuben who spoke first. "What the hell do you want Logan, you're violating the restraining order!" "To HELL with the restraining order!" he screamed. "Like I said, I told you that I was going to make your life miserable!" He directed his attention toward Kashi, who said, "Logan what are you talking about? You know that it's over between us. You're delusional and crazy!" "Shut up bitch! This is between me and your nigger friend, Reuben! he spat.

Reuben jerked his hand from Kashi's grip to confront Logan face to face. "Kashi go and get in the car," he demanded. "NO! I'm not leaving you! Logan please don't do this!" she pleaded but her requests fell on deaf ears. Reuben moved Kashi to the side and Logan took a step towards him. "Bring it on, you bastard!" Reuben challenged. Logan was just inches away from Reuben's face and you could tell things were becoming very serious. Logan then said, "I can see you've been caught in Kashi's web just like everyone else and I hate to disappoint you but there's only room for two of us in her web and that's me and Kashi and if I can't have her, you certainly won't!" Logan then lunged at Reuben and knocked him to the ground. Reuben got up and charged at Logan causing both men to fall. Kashi stood in the background screaming, pleading and yelling for both of them to stop but the fight continued. They proceeded to kick and punch one another, while rolling on the ground. Kashi grabbed her cell phone from her purse and shakily dialed 911. "911 operator may I help you?" "YES!" Kashi screamed. "Please send the police to Seaside Lake right away! There are two men fighting and I think they may kill each other!" Kashi was in the middle of her sentence, when she saw Logan pull something black and shiny out of his pocket. The two of them were still struggling on the ground when the quiet of the night was interrupted by two gunshots. She heard one of them moaning but she couldn't tell who it was. "Were those shots fired?" asked the operator. "YES, PLEASE HURRY! Kashi screamed. "The police are on the way ma'am" Kashi threw her phone to the ground and watched in horror, as Reuben fell backwards and Logan struggled to get up. He made it to his feet but Reuben grabbed Logan's ankle and tripped him. Logan fell to the ground face down, causing the gun to fly out of his hand. He tried to crawl towards the gun but Reuben was too fast for him. He reached past Logan and managed to grab it. As Logan reached for Reuben's neck, Reuben fired the gun twice. Logan grabbed his chest and his eyes widened, as he realized he had been shot.

Somehow, he managed to stand up and stagger towards the water. The last thing that Kashi and Reuben witnessed was Logan falling face down into the lake. Breathless and in pain, Reuben watched in horror, as Logan's body floated away with the tide.

Reuben slumped over and let the relief of unconsciousness over take him. Kashi cried hysterically, as she fell to her knees to cradle Reuben. Blood was everywhere and she knew that both men had shot each other. She heard the sirens in the distance and soon was surrounded by several policemen and EMT Technicians but in her heart, she knew it was now too late.

One year later

She was absolutely adorable and looked like both of her parents. She giggled and cooed as she tried to walk on her own but it was no use. She kept falling and laughing and trying over and over again. As Kashi watched her daughter half walk and half crawl, she knew that she was a blessed woman. Aria was the best gift that Reuben could have given her. They chose the name Aria because it was similar to Kashi's sister- in- law, Ariel. She wiped tears of joy away, as she watched her daughter play. She glanced over her shoulder and saw Reuben cooking on the grill. They had chosen a wonderful day to spend at the park. So much was now behind them, yet so much lay ahead.

Reuben had suffered a flesh wound that night, a year ago and Kashi had feared the worst. She thought that Reuben had died. The day after the shooting, Kashi had gone into stress induced labor and delivered Aria. Two months later, Kashi and Reuben were married in a small ceremony as planned with Reuben's family present and Kashi's best friend, Monisha. Kashi was very sad that her family still wanted nothing to do with her. Even when Monisha had informed them of the birth of their grandchild, they still chose not to forgive.

Logan's body was never discovered. Rescuers and dive teams combed the lake for months afterwards and no signs of Dr. Logan Roy had ever been found. The authorities were sure that he had been shot but were uncertain as to whether he had survived. The story made headline news for weeks and months but eventually the case was closed.

Life in general had seemed to settle down and the ghosts of the past had seemed to die. However, on occasion, that eerie feeling would wash over Kashi. The feeling that she was being watched. The feeling that something was not quite right.

And now as she looked over her shoulder into the wooded area of the park, she was reminded of that dreadful night. She walked over to Reuben and he took her in his arms. He kissed her forehead and held her. She buried her face in the warmth of his chest, feeling safe and secure if only for a moment. But somehow she had the feeling that they were still being watched..........

Imari Rogan

CPSIA information can be obtained
at www.ICGtesting.com
Printed in the USA
FFHW021452021118
49228557-53444FF